Praise for Simon Crump

'A deliciously obscene and
King ... Think Quentin Tarantino on acid in Graceland ...
Extraordinary'
Sunday Times on *My Elvis Blackout*

'There's no way out from Crump's disturbing grip'
Scotsman

Like an episode of *South Park*, where just as you get into the story something goes splat, Crump's contorted imagination is alarmingly enjoyable'
Guardian on *My Elvis Blackout*

'Simon Crump is a cult classic in the making'
Scotland on Sunday

'Primary school prose and a plot out of a cokehead's arse ... This book is a waste of paper'
TNT magazine on *My Elvis Blackout*

'Here's a book to really make you laugh, providing you have a tough constitution'
Big Issue on *My Elvis Blackout*

'Crump writes with such a lack of fear that it's both hilariously refreshing and destined to gloriously offend any fans who prefer to forget his amphetamine-stuffed cheeseburger death'
FHM on *My Elvis Blackout*

NEVERLAND

NEVERLAND

Simon Crump

First published in 2009 by Old Street Publishing Ltd
40 Bowling Green Lane, London EC1R 0BJ
www.oldstreetpublishing.co.uk

ISBN 978-1-905847-37-2

Copyright © Simon Crump 2009

The right of Simon Crump to be identified as the author of this work has been asserted by him in accordance with the Copyright, Designs and Patents Act 1988.

All rights reserved. No part of this publication may be reproduced, stored in or introduced into a retrieval system, or transmitted, in any form, or by any means (electronic, mechanical, photocopying, recording or otherwise) without the prior written permission of the publisher.

10 9 8 7 6 5 4 3 2 1

A CIP catalogue record for this title is available from the British Library.

Printed and bound in Great Britain.

For Tracey, George and Maria

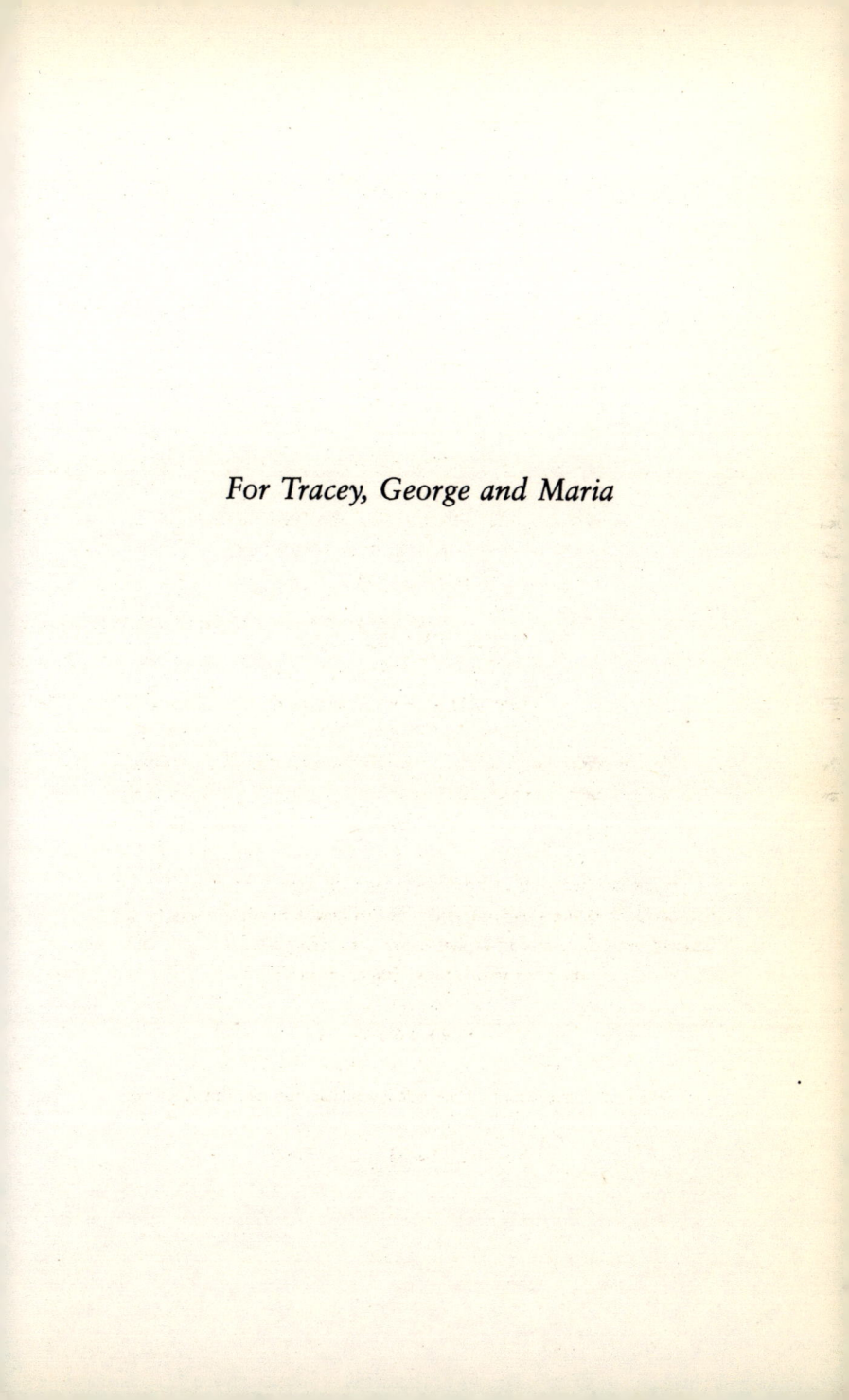

'So the white crook-neck thing, white too about the wattles, stood around grabbing what and whenever it could, but sort of sideways.'

'Why're the others pecking at it, Pa?'

'Because they don't like the look of it. Because it's different.'

Patrick White, *The Vivisector*

Fumes

We watched the coffin slip away and stood silent as the workmen began to cover the hole with concrete.

'Fuck,' Marty said. 'He's gone. So what are we supposed to do now? I ain't trained to do anything but look after him.'

Elvis's death fucked up everyone's life. Thought I'd better leave the plan before the plan left me.

I went home to Mary, my wife of thirty-one years. She'd left me a note on the hall stand: 'Dear Lamar, I just fell out of love with you,' it read. 'I am at my sisiter's place.'

'Sisiter's,' I thought. She means sister's.

She'd waited till the kids were grown. I couldn't blame her for leavin me. At best I am very hard to live with.

I got drunk and I stayed drunk for a week. I spent

the rest of the summer pumpin gas. Come fall, I got so pissed with the smell of the gas and diesel and the left-arm-tan shit-heads laughin in my face that I answered one of them dumb 'life-changing' job ads in the Press Scimitar.

I went for interview in a rented office over a corner hardware store, nothin fancy. The interview-Broad fixed me a real nasty-tastin coffee and asked me a list of dumb questions about my 'interpersonal skills'. Knowin how to order a limo isn't a strong qualification for anythin.

I ignored the questions and told her a bunch of stories about my time with Elvis, true most of 'em.

'We'll get back to you Lamar,' she said.

'Yeah, course you will,' I said.

'Your doubt is your undoing,' she said. Biblical like. I went home, called up the gas station and quit the job anyway, couldn't stand them damned fumes a fuckin minute longer. I fixed myself a nice steak dinner. I was too damned tired to eat it. I slept. I dreamt about teachin a dog to ride a bicycle.

I woke up in the mornin and my mouth felt like somethin had passed away on my palate, and boy did I need the bathroom. First thing I notice is there ain't no water in the john and the bulb is out. So I go downstairs. The power to the whole house is down and there ain't no water in the pipes neither.

The plates in the kitchen sink are green and the food in the Frigidaire is rotten. I just sat down there and I cried. No power, no water, no nothin. And my best friend is dead.

I pulled on my mauve nylon slacks, splashed on the Aqua Manda and eased into my yellow hide sports coat. I checked myself in the full-length mirror. Lookin tired, lookin old, Lamar, and in bad need of a shave, I thought. But still 250lbs of fine-looking *hombre*.

I went down to the lobby, and boy was I popular today. I'd never seen so much mail.

I hauled open the front door and stepped out onto the street. I looked around. It all felt kinda different, even a tad odd. The old neighbourhood was the same but it felt strange – couldn't get a handle on it, but it felt different. I felt like people were starin. I walked the two blocks down to the little Mom & Pops grocery store I went to every mornin and damn me it was gone. In its place there was 'Colins Convenience 24-7 Point & Pay'.

I picked out a few supplies and took them over to the counter. I couldn't get over the prices these motherfuckers were chargin.

The chick at the checkout had a jagged red streak

in her hair, metal in her face and padded shoulders like a damn football player.

She peered at me over the top of the supermarket tabloid she was readin.

'Yes?'

'These few meagre comestibles and I'll take a pack of Hav-A-Tampa Jewels if you'd be so good, ma'am.'

While she reached behind the counter for my cigars I checked out the checkout chick's newspaper headline.

ELVIS IS ALIVE!!
SIXTEEN YEARS AFTER HIS 'DEATH' ELVIS HAS BEEN SIGHTED ON A GOLF COURSE IN MONTANA.

'Montana?' I thought.
'Golf?'
'Montana?'
'Sixteen years?'
'Golf is shit.'

And then it hit me quicker than a New York second. I'd been out cold for sixteen straight years.

Must have been them gas fumes I guess.

Gold

Michael was born with gold in his mouth.
 He left his mom without too much trouble. He shimmied out. The midwife held him in her white-gloved grip. She struck his face and a shining nugget plopped onto the soiled sheets of the birthing table. He sang and he danced. He bit off his cord. He slipped on a white glove of his own and signed a few autographs.
 'We love you Michael,' they all said.
 'I love you more,' he said back.
 They called a priest. After all, a minute-old baby isn't supposed to act that way.
 'Where is the gold?' he cried. 'Where is the gold??'

For a while there was gold, lots of it, and there were cartoons and songs and dance and lunar walking and Motown and I want you back.
 We fixed him though. Then we fucked him. And we took it all.

Uri?

'The boy is grown now and I did my time. With my brown hair going grey and my broken heart. I still miss her. And crazy as it might seem I'm still very much in love.'

'That's nice, Uri.' Michael said. 'I didn't understand it but it was nice.'

'Thank you, Michael.'

'Well listen, Uri, I want to do some talking now. Can I ask you a sort of personal question?'

'Go ahead, Michael. I can't promise that I'll answer it, but you can ask it.'

Michael picked up a biscuit, broke it neatly in half and laid the halves back on the plate.

His eyes grew a shade darker.

'Well it's about you and Susan.'

'Susan? I don't know any Susan.'

'Sorry, Uri, that's not the question I meant to ask.'

Michael looked at Uri then looked quickly away.

He picked up another biscuit, broke it neatly in half and laid the halves back on the plate.

There was a short silence, filled only by the muted hum of the Frigidaire.

Forget it, Uri.'

'Michael. Listen, what's bothering you? Tell me.'

Michael looked sadly at the plate of unbroken biscuits.

'Uri, I'm thirty-five now and my mother said...'

'Your mother? Mothers don't know everything. What did she say?'

Michael picked up another biscuit.

'What did she say, Michael? What did your mother say?'

Michael broke the biscuit neatly in half and laid the two halves back on the plate.

'She told me not to worry. Anyway how's your beard, Uri? I hear you've got a new electeric razor? They tell me... they tell me you plug it in wherever you go.'

'Electric, Michael. Not electeric, electric.'

Michael picked up another biscuit, broke it neatly in half and laid the halves back on the plate.

His eyes grew a shade darker.

There was a short silence filled only with the muted hum of the Frigidaire and the angry buzzing of Uri's electric razor.

Fumes

I called Mary up at her sister's.

'ComebacktomeMary,' I said weepin.

'OK,' she said. 'But we gotta get out of Memphis.'

We lit out for California, to a little place called Los Olivos 'bout 100 miles north of LA. Mary had family out there; an elder sister who ran an art gallery and a brother-in-law, Frank, who owned a gas station and van conversion plant.

It was all settled. We were to visit with them temporary, Mary would help her sister out at the gallery and Frank agreed to set me on as gopher at the garage. My main duty was pumpin gas.

Two months along the way Mary and me moved into our own place, a 24 x 60 foot mobile home on the Breezy Point Farm Trailer Park on Flying Flags Drive, right off Highway 154. It wasn't much, but it was ours and Mary and me were back together again. Sometimes her face lit up just for me.

I liked it there, kinda reminded me of my old trailer out back at Graceland and the good times with Elvis and the guys.

Three days later a gold Chrysler New Yorker swung into Frank's gas station. The Broad from the job interview got out. At first I thought it must be them damn gas fumes and that I'm hallucinatin but it really was the same Broad. She came over.

She'd finally got back to me.

'You got the job,' she says. 'Month's try-out. Go easy on the cussing.'

'Fuckin awesome... Great,' I say. 'When do I start?'

'You already did,' she says. 'Get in.'

We drove out through the rollin hills of the Santa Ynez Valley and hit the Figueroa Mountain Road. I asked the woman how she'd found me. She told me to mind my own business.

'From now on you do exactly as I say, Lamar,' she said. 'I tell you what to think, when to think and how to think it.'

We passed a few real nice-lookin horse ranches and then the Broad pulled the wheel hard over. She hung a right and we motored down a long gravel drive flanked by oak trees until we came upon a high wooden fence with 'No Trespassing' signs posted every few yards. The fence gave out to a section of stone wall covered in orange ivy, then the Chrysler pulled up at a pair of tall wooden gates with steel grilles.

The Broad leaned out of the Chrysler and spoke into a little birdhouse.

Somethin inside the birdhouse crackled and a man's voice said, 'Ok.'

The gates swung open and we were in.

First thing that caught my attention was a giraffe, then after that an elephant. And then some kinda messed-up tall sheep thing with a long neck.

'What in the name of fuck is that?' I asked the Broad.

'It's a Llama,' she said.

'Do I like Llamas?' I asked her.

'You decide, Lamar,' she said.

We come up to a house. It kinda looked like Disney World to me.

'When you meet your new employer,' the Broad said, 'Please tell him that you are a true and dedicated fan and that you love him a lot.'

'Sure.' I said.

She turned to me with a broad smile and I realise it's the first time I've ever seen the Broad smile.

Real pretty she looked.

'Lamar?'

'Yes ma'am?'

'Are you ready for fun on a grand scale?'

A maid let us in. She directed us through a pine-panelled lobby around twenty times the size of my trailer and motioned us towards an overstuffed six-seater yellow leather couch with a lattice work base. You coulda kept chickens in it if you'd wanted.

A panel slid back and Lisa stepped right out of the wall.

'Hey Lamar,' she said. 'Long time, huh?'

Boy was she grown and boy, did she look like her daddy.

Golden Days

Previously, fruits were very cheap so people who used to eat them would senselessly litter the place with their skins and pips, but now fruit is expensive so there is little wastage.

Before, you could buy, with one piece, a dozen oranges, a dozen bananas, half a dozen custard apples, two dozen mangoes, half a dozen pineapples, a whole bunch of lychees of two kinds (the Chinese and the local), a small basket of guavas (*mapera*), about three sticks of sugar cane, a lemon and a jackfruit the size of a three-year-old child.

But that is all in the past.

The golden days are gone.

Kings of America

This real funny-lookin chick comes prancin down the hall carryin a tray with four soft-drink bottles balanced on it.

She sets it down on the marble-top coffee table and flashes me a proper friendly smile.

I check her out. Pale skin, long black hair, red lipstick.

'So how do you like my home?' she says. 'I was going to put them in glasses. The refreshments I mean, but I couldn't find any in the kitchen. Glasses I mean. How about I just say everything backwards from now on?' She laughs. 'I've been away so long I was lucky to even find the kitchen. I was lucky to find the kitchen I've been away so long.'

Make no mistake, she was funny all right and I liked her right off.

Then she slips her arm around Lisa and kisses her full on the mouth.

Seen a lot of degenerate shit in my time let me tell ya, but I never had Lisa figured for albino pussy.

'I made love to Lisa in my Mickey Mouse pyjamas,' she says. 'And then I asked her to marry me. One day she's going to give me a little boy of my own.'

And now I'm guessin what Elvis would have made of all this, thinkin how he'd have busted right out of his tomb and tried every which way to get up here to the happy valley and slap the shit out of the both of them.

'Lamar, this is my fiancée,' Lisa says. 'Would you please stop staring please, Lamar, and say hello to Michael.'

The Broad shoots me an old-fashioned look and I start to get to grips with the sketch.

'Oh... Hi... Michelle, I just want to tell ya that I am a true and dedicated fan and that I love her a lot.'

'"You,"' says the Broad.

'I am a true and dedicated fan Michelle and I love YOU a lot.' I say with feelin.

'It's Michael,' the funny-lookin chick says. 'Not Michelle. Although I quite like that. To be known as Michelle would be, well, simply... magical. I've heard a lot about you, Lamar, and I'm expecting you're a little nervous. I'm sure you've heard all my albums and you know just how big a star I really am?'

'Hey Michael, sorry,' I say. 'I just want to say that I am a true and dedicated fan and that I love you a lot.'

He takes my hand.

'So you've heard all my albums?'

'Yeah... I mean no... I mean, I mean sorry man. I mean I slept. Elvis died. Mary left me. I slept. I got this shitty job in a gas station. I slept.'

Michael turns to the Broad. The Broad who got me into all this shit in the first place. The Broad with the real pretty smile who tells me when to think and what to think and how to think it.

'You gave him coffee then?' he simpers.

'I sure did, Michael. Slow acting. I needed time to think,' she says. 'We needed downtime. Lamar needed downtime.'

Sixteen fuckin years I'm thinking?

Sixteen fuckin years downtime?

Sixteen fuckin years?

'You got a bathroom in this Disney joint Michael?'

'In actual fact Lamar, I have thirty bathrooms in this house,' he says. 'Simply... magical isn't it?'

I find myself in bathroom number one. Shed a few tears. Splash some water on my face. Freshen up a tad. Sixteen fuckin years I think. Then I check myself in the mirror. Bad need of shave, loud shirt, yellow-hide sports coat, mauve nylon slacks, but still 250lbs of one damn fine-lookin *hombre*.

Hey ho, I figure. Screw my little plans. These are the breaks.

Then I go back to Michael, Lisa and the Broad who fuckin drugged me and I start over.

Michael

We went up to this girl in't' street. Right nice she looked. Tight black top. A bloke with her. Ancient. He must have been about 35. Ancient he was. With smiling disease.

Anyway, we went up to this girl and we showed her us bikes and she smiled.

'They're good bikes,' she said.

'We're all men,' I said.

Moon

Elvis called me 'moon'. I have a bald spot.

He offered to buy me a Hollywood hairpiece one time but I never accepted his offer on account of the fact that I knew one of the guys would have torn the damned thing offa my head in front of Miss Traffic Safety or the Queen of England or some other such shit.

I colour the bald spot over with a magic marker. Ridiculous, I know. But I do it anyway. Then I comb it over.

I have to admit to usin hairspray.

I sat down on the couch with Michael and Lisa. I said we had to get this whole scenario clear. That we had to lay out some ground rules. I acted the tough guy and struck a match on the zip of my slacks, just like I'd seen Elvis do a thousand times. I lit up a Hav-A-Tampa Jewel and tossed the match over my shoulder.

My whole head flashed.

Must have overdone it with the Silvikrin I guess.

Anyway, so I sat there for a moment, actin tough, hopin neither of them two crazy kids would notice that my head was ablaze. Act natural I figured, like it happens all the time.

Michael panicked when the fire started and he up and ran. Lisa turned on me.

'You fucking idiot!' she yelled. 'Now look what you've done. You've upset Michael!'

She took off after him.

I rolled off of the couch and prostrated myself on the rug, tryin to pull it around me to smother the fire. The flames shot across the rug and began climbin the heavy velvet drapes either side of the French windows. Pretty soon the whole goddam room was afire.

When I came to, I was lyin in a hospital bed and Michael was bendin over me.

'That was the wiggiest goof of them all,' he says. 'You are one super funny guy, Lamar.'

I stared at him in sudden fear. I couldn't answer.

Somethin seemed to have closed up in my throat and I couldn't unlock it.

'That's a nasty burn on your scalp,' he said. 'Same thing happened to me once.'

I swallowed hard. Wet the inside of my lips. Forced myself to speak.

'I just want to tell you that I am a true and dedicated fan and that I love you a lot,' I croaked.

'Here,' Michael said, handin me a brand new black fedora. 'You'll be needing this.'

Michael

When I were young I were a big fan of arson.

Mostly I smelled like a spent firework. Molten plastic Zoob Zoobs were my thing.

I were out on 10-acre field watching a goose repeatedly bite my sister Janet's arse. I were top man that day, full box of Scottish Bluebell in my pocket and a roll of bin-bags stuffed down front of me jeans. Summer and all that. I decided to fire the grass embankment.

Found the best stick ever. Dry as stick it were and it made a top medieval torch. Wrapped it in bin bags and fired it up. Applied it to a patch of yellow grass and ran like fuck. Watched the rolling inferno devour the embankment.

Went back and heard the faint cry of things in

pain. Frogs. Hundreds of them. Worst thing was, most of them were still alive.

I moved amongst them with a stick weeping uncontrollably.

I know I'll go to hell for that performance.

Friends

We're out on the terrace overlookin the big floral clock drinkin iced tea.

The four of us. Michael, Lisa, the Broad and me.

There's Disney music comin out of fibreglass rocks in the rose beds and way off in the distance I can hear the screams of children ridin the Ferris wheel in Michael's private amusement park. As far as you can see there are rollin green hills, regimented vineyards and dense scented copses of western red cedar.

It sure is pretty.

'Real nice place you got here, Michael.' I say.

'Thuuuuuuuur Lumuur,' he says.

'Scuse me?'

'Michael said *thank you Lamar*,' Lisa says.

'U buu yu wuuuuuuuuun whu cur hur tuuuuuuur?' Michael says.

'Pardon me Michael?'

The Broad shoots me a look. She seems a tad annoyed.

'Michael just said, Lamar,' the Broad snaps, '*I bet you're wondering why I've called you here today?*'

'Wuuuu muu uuu huu cuuuuu tuu huuu us buu... uh,' Michael says.

'Jesus fuckin Christ... I mean I'm sorry man.'

'Michael said,' Lisa says crossly, '*We're meeting out here because the house is bugged.* Look, Lamar, we understand him. How come you don't?'

'I'm sorry ma'am, guess I'm just not used to it just yet. Acclimatised like.'

'Whuuuu yuu luuu tu tuuuuu tuuu uhhh?' Michael says.

'Listen Michael, I sure am sorry about this.'

'Lamar, you dumb deaf fuck,' the Broad yells. 'Michael says *would you like him to take his mask off?*'

'Yes Michael. If you would...'

Michael removes his gorilla mask. Underneath it he's wearin a blue surgical mask and mirrored aviator shades. Just like the ones Elvis always wore.

'I love it when people stop and are scared,' he says. 'And I love it when they don't know that it's me inside the mask. I love it. It's simply... magical.'

'OK, Michael, I got all of that. Every single damn word.'

Lisa and the Broad smile and the atmosphere improves somewhat. We can all be friends again.

'Tell Lamar about the time at the airport,' Lisa grins. 'When you were wearing your gorilla mask and you tripped over a sand-filled ashtray and fell on the floor in a heap in front of all those photographers.'

'Do I have to, Lisa?' he giggles.

'Yes you do, sweetheart.'

'Oh Lamar, it was so funny. One time I was at the airport when I was wearing my gorilla mask and I tripped over a sand-filled ashtray and fell on the floor in a heap in front of all these photographers. It was simply… awful.'

'So what's with the emergency-room mask Michael if you don't mind me askin?'

'I had my wisdom teeth taken out, for my voice you know. Oh man you can't believe what I've been going through.'

'Sounds simply… awful,' I say

'Don't push it, Lamar.' Michael says. Dry like.

He adjusts the red armband on his black military jacket, squeals and grabs his crotch.

'Now shall we get to business?'

'Sure, Michael.'

Motown

As we sat in the Motown boardroom eating a nicely catered lunch, I began to think more seriously about my life and decided to put God at the top of my list of priorities.

Don't be duped. It isn't trendy to go against your conscience. Or try to impress with a cool image. Sometimes I dream that God defecates on my chest. Sometimes I wonder how he found the time to terrify all the demons. And sometimes I ask myself how tough it's going to be to commit myself to a programme of pure living, self-denial and sacrifice.

I gave up smoking and then I gave up violence.

Fullerton Avenue Underpass

So Michael tells me the plan. He says he has his own private army who call themselves the Soldiers Of Love or some such dumb name. They've seen The Fullerton Avenue Underpass Virgin Mary Holy Saltwater Run-Off Stain on CBS News and taken it as a sign.

Michael says they'll all head down to Memphis, break into a Mausoleum, cut through a wrought iron door and then hit the crypt. They'll drill a hole in a nine-hundred-pound casket, screw in an eyebolt and use a hand winch to pull the casket out. Then they load the thing into the Gold Chrysler New Yorker and transfer it to a refrigerator in the Amour meat packin house.

From there it goes back to Los Olivos.

Michael says he's worked it all out in detail and

that he will lead the operation disguised in his *Toysasaurus* Spiderman costume, that the Broad will drive, and that I will act as head of security.

He says I can wear what I like.

My best friend is dead. And Michael wants to take his body.

'Why in the name of Fuck would you want to do this, Michael?' I ask calmly.

'As wedding present for Lisa, Lamar,' he says. 'I already have the Elephant Man and I couldn't get to Jesus. The King is the next best thing. Plus I'd like Lisa to have her daddy at the wedding.'

I took Michael by the throat and I called him a sonofabitch and everythin else. And the weirdest thing was he began laughin at me. I set him down gentle like and went outside into the garden. Got all cosy amongst the damn rose trees. I pushed my brand new black fedora way back on my achin head and lit myself a Hav-A-Tampa Jewel. There was a rustle behind me and I felt somebody standin there. I whipped around all ready to sock their lights out.

It was the Broad.

'Hey Lamar,' she said. 'You Ok? I brought you a cup of coffee.'

I woke up in the long grass behind the shower block at the Breezy Point Farm Maximum Stay Trailer Park. Boy did my head hurt.

She took my hat. That bitch took my hat. My only present from Michael.

I crawled back to my trailer.

There was a note from Mary on the kitchen counter.

'Lamar, I just fell out of love with you,' it read.

I phoned Mary at her sister's. She wasn't there.

Uri??

Michael ran his hands through his hair. He looked at Uri wildly.

He picked up a biscuit, broke it neatly in half and laid the halves back on the plate.

His eyes grew a shade darker.

'Well listen, Uri, I want to do some talking now. Can I ask you a sort of personal question?'

'Go ahead, Michael. I can't promise that I'll answer it, but you can ask it.'

Michael picked up a biscuit. His eyes shining with unshed tears.

'Uri... Uri...'
 'Yes?'
 'Uri... No I can't.'

Michael pushed the plate away from him, broke the biscuit neatly in half and laid the halves on the table.

His eyes grew a shade darker.

'Uri?'
'Michael?'
'No I can't. I just can't...'

Michael pulled the plate towards him. He picked up another biscuit.

'OK, Uri... No I can't.'
'Yes you can.'
'OK, Uri... No, no sorry. I can't'
'For goodness' sake, Michael, just ask me the question.'

Michael's eyes welled over. The biscuit crumbled, made flaccid by the flow of his tears. Soggy fragments littered the table.

'Uri. My hair is never "just right on the night". At dances I admire the sheen of other boys' hair. Mine is drab and lifeless. Janet told me about egg shampoo, but I found it messy to use.'

'The secret of egg shampoo, Michael, is to use tepid and not hot water, otherwise you'll have scrambled egg shampoo. Beat the yolks and whites of two eggs separately, then fold them in together. Wet the hair with tepid water, massage half the shampoo into the scalp, rinse and repeat with the remainder. A course of six weekly egg shampoos will show a decided improvement.'

Michael picked up a biscuit, broke it neatly in half and laid the halves back on the plate.

His eyes grew a shade darker.

A maid came into the room. She wiped the table.

There was a short silence, filled only by the muted hum of the Frigidaire.

Tito

'The Bible's in two parts,' Pauline says.

'Fuck off,' we say.

'What's that?' she says.

'Fuck off,' we both say. 'That's in two parts an' all, Pauline. Fuck and Off.'

'Who taught you to say such bad things?' Pauline says.

'Dad did,' we say.

I'm nine so I know about life and all this stuff but my brother Michael's only seven and he knows fuck all about fuck all. Dad always said to us, he always said, he warned us did Dad, if anybody starts talking about the Bible, starts trying to shove Jesus Christ up your arse you just tell 'em, tell 'em to get 'emselves fucked off.

'So can I tell you about the Bible?' Pauline says.

'No.'

'Michael? Tito? Are you sure?'

'Fuck off.'

Dad read me out my school report. 'It says here,' he says, '*Tito is perfectly capable of behaving himself if he wants to, but sometimes he chooses not to behave himself and messes about on the mat instead.*'

'I've changed, Dad,' I told him. 'I've changed.'

'You've what, Tito?'

'I've changed, Dad, I've really changed. There is no more silliness in my heart.'

Motown

Michael worked hard at his part-time job as a delivery boy for his local Chinese takeaway.

He'd answered an advertisement he'd seen in the post office which read 'Wanted – Delivery Diver'. They got it sorted, even had a reet old laugh about the unfortunate typographical error.

Michael changed out of his frogman's suit and flippers and packed them in the trunk of his red 1979 Mustang, which was in perfect nick. Michael sometimes earned as much as sixty quid in one night and often referred to himself as 'the best delivery diver in South Yorkshire'.

Despite the vast sums of money which Michael lavished on the Mustang, he had managed to save three thousand quid by the start of his final year at the tech.

'Fuck this,' Michael thought one day and bought himself a train ticket to Motown, day return. He sang a song for Mester Berry Gordy. Blew his brains clean out the back of his skull.

'You're booked, Sunshine,' said Berry. 'That were champion. You've got a reet gob on yer. And tha knows 'ow to curl thee voice.'

'Nice one pal,' Michael said. 'Correct. Tha's double reet about that Mester Gordy.'

Gordy leaned forward in his chair. Ground his big cigar into a cut glass ashtray.

'Now then, love... let's record summat the kids can finally have a proper fuckin dance to.'

Oh yes.

Andrew

I've been on six twelve-hour night shifts and sad as this may seem your party has been the end of my tunnel. Not everyone lives his or her life alone and for a little while it seems my whole world is all right.

    He's special and he doesn't speak. Every day for sixteen years he leaves the flat and he gets a paper. One day he gets a paper and he also points at some mints.

    The woman behind the counter finally cracks.

    'If you could talk, Andrew, what would you say?'

eBay

Four years passed before the gold Chrysler New Yorker pulled up in front of my trailer.

The Broad got out and handed me a brand new black fedora.

'He finally forgave you, Lamar,' the Broad says. 'After all this time.'

'Look, lady, I ain't too sure about this.'

'He wants you back. You know? Like in the record. He didn't want you around, but now he wants you back. He got you a new hat and everything. You OK with that?'

'I ain't got no place else to go, lady,' I say. 'My Mary left me. My best friend is dead.'

'We're in touch with Mary, Lamar,' the Broad says. 'She still loves you.'

'Where is she? Where is my Mary?'

'Closer than you think, Lamar. You'll be with her anytime soon.'

We drove out through the rollin hills of the Santa Ynez Valley and hit the Figueroa Mountain Road.

We passed a few real nice-lookin horse ranches and then the Broad pulled the wheel hard over. She hung a right and we motored down the long gravel drive flanked by oak trees until we came upon the high wooden fence with 'No Trespassing' signs posted every few yards. The fence gave out to a section of stone wall covered in orange ivy, then the Chrysler pulled up to the tall wooden gates with steel grilles.

The Broad leaned out of the Chrysler and spoke into the birdhouse.

Somethin inside the birdhouse crackled and a man's voice said, 'OK.'

The gates swung open and we were in.

The giraffe was still there and so was the elephant. And the messed-up tall sheep thing with the long neck.

'Did you decide about the Llama, Lamar?' the Broad asks.

'Lady, I hate them fuckin long neck things, OK?'

We go into the pine-panelled lobby and he's there. Waitin.

'You hurt my neck, Lamar,' Michael whimpers.

'I wanted to sing "She's a dancing machine", but it came out "She's mean to sheep". You hurt me, Lamar. It affected my voice. I had to have surgery. It was simply...'

'Yeah I know, Mike. It was simply... painful. I fuckin hope.'

'Nobody calls me Mike, Lamar.'

'Yeah, well I do from here on in, Mike. I'm so fuckin bored with sayin two syllables Michael. And if you ever, ever, try to pull an Elvis stunt like that again, you will wake up one mornin and find yourself fuckin dead. You got that, one-syllable Mike?'

'Lamar, you are so funny. You are the coolest!'

'Yeah I know, Mike. Always have been. And you got more shit in you than a Christmas goose. So what can I do for you today, Mike?'

'I want you to head up security for me and I want us both to have fun. In this house boys have rights. You are my best buddy, Lamar. And we're both boys yeah? The coolest.'

'Sure, Mike.'

'You ever heard of the Internet, Lamar?'

'Yeah. No not really, Mike. Kinda passed me by. Elvis died. I got a shitty job in a gas station. I met your mystery Broad. I slept.'

Mike then delivers me a short and informative lecture about the goddamn information superhighway. Brung it to my attention there's a piece of peripheral hardware called a modem, a gizmo that enables other users to communicate with each other over the telephone lines. Chew the shit and shoot the fat with folks all over the territory without havin to speak to 'em direct like so he says. Sorta like a computer party line. Then he tells me all about an auction site called eBay.

When he's through my goddamn head is spinnin but I kinda get it.

'You got all that, Lamar?' He asks.

'Yeah, Mike, my goddamn head is spinnin but I kinda get it.'

'Ok good. See, I told you it would be fun. You having fun, Lamar?'

'Yeah. Kinda, Mike.'

'You know anything about unicorns, Lamar?'

'A little, Mike. I know about that real nice picture where the gentle and pensive Virgin Mary chick has the power to tame the unicorn. It's a fresco actually, in Palazzo Farnese Rome, Italy, probably done by Domenichino around 1602.'

'Yes, Lamar, that's right. It is a magical painting. I'm going to buy it one day.'

'It's a fresco, Mike, not a paintin. There is a fuckin difference.'

'Anyway, Lamar, medieval knowledge of the fabulous beast stems from biblical and ancient sources, and the creature was variously represented as a kind of wild ass, goat, or horse. By A.D. 200, Tertullian had called the unicorn "a small, fierce, kidlike animal, a symbol of Christ". Saints Ambrose, Jerome, and Basil agreed. The predecessor of the medieval bestiary, compiled in Late Antiquity and known as *Physiologus* popularized an elaborate allegory in which a unicorn, trapped by a maiden (representing the Virgin Mary) stood for the Incarnation. As soon as the unicorn sees her it lays its head on her lap and falls asleep. This became a basic emblematic tag that underlies medieval notions of the unicorn, justifying its appearance in every form of religious art.

In popular belief, examined wittily and at length by Sir Thomas Browne in his *Pseudodoxia Epidemica*, unicorn horns could neutralize poisons. Therefore, people who feared poisoning sometimes drank from goblets made of "unicorn horn". Alleged aphrodisiac qualities and other purported medicinal virtues also drove up the cost of "unicorn" products such as milk, hide, and offal. Unicorns were also said to be able to determine whether or not a woman was a virgin; in some tales, they could only be mounted by virgins.'

'Yeah, sure, Mike,' I say. 'I take your point, and "emblematic tag" sure is a nice phrase for a young kid such as yourself to be usin at this point in your discourse, but you must remember that with the rise of humanism, the unicorn also acquired positive secular meanings, includin chaste love and faithful marriage. It plays this role in Petrarch's *Triumph of Chastity*. And if you disagree with that in anyway whatsoever Mike, I'm here to tell you, buddy, that I will sock yer fuckin lights out.'

'You are the coolest, Lamar!'

'Anyway Mike?' I say. 'So what's all this shit got to do with anythin?'

'Well you know my plan... The wedding present, the one concerning Lisa's daddy? The one that got you so riled-up.?'

'Yeah. Don't even go there, boy.'

'Well... I had another idea Lamar. For our anniversary. I'm going to get Lisa a unicorn, off eBay. Shall we go upstairs and log on?'

We climb the windin marble stairway right to the top of the house.

Michael's bedroom is dark; the windows blacked out just the way Elvis always liked it. The only light in the room comes from his computer monitor. He's got a Three Stooges screensaver.

We sit at his desk and as my eyes get used to the gloom I realise.

Holy shit! There's people in here. A whole damn row of 'em crammed against one wall.

'What in the name of Fuck are all these folks doin up here Mike?'

'They're my friends, Lamar. Put the light on if you want and say hello.'

So I put the lights on. Michael's bedroom is large and cluttered. Not dirty or anythin, just untidy. Some of the walls are covered with cloth and there's gold records and pictures of Peter Pan everywhere. In one corner of the room there's a child's crib with a chimp asleep in it. And then I really get to check out his friends. Shop dummies. Five of 'em. Full size plastic people dressed in military jackets, white buckskin jodhpurs and black fedora hats. Just like mine and Mike's.

'What's with the dummies, Mike?'

'Mannequins, Lamar, mannequins. This room is my favourite place on earth. I guess that someday I want to bring those mannequins to life. And I like to imagine talking to them. They're my friends. They don't ask me questions.'

Michael logs on. He hits the eBay site and pretty soon we're sat down together like father and son scrollin through all the shit.

He's a nice kid. And as I sit by him I wish I had a son of my own and we were shoppin for fishin equipment, slot cars, baseball gloves, and bubblegum cards. Or best of all gifts for my Mary.

Michael double clicks on a listin and a picture comes up. A real nice white pony six hands high, good legs and a single spiral horn on its forehead.

'Genuine California Unicorn' it reads. 'Seeks careful owner. Must go to good home. Buy it now. Two million dollars. Free shipping.'

'Can we get it, Lamar? Can we get it? Can we? Can we? Can we?' he squeals.

'Sure we can, son,' I say.

And then Michael hits the 'Buy Now' button.

He gets a message straight back. 'Congratulations! You won the item. Delivery will be in three hours.'

We hang out by the pool. The kid's clearly overexcited and vulnerable as a bubble in a nut factory.

I hear a horn sound at the gates and I walk down there. I hook up with the gateman and introduce myself as the new head of security. He seems like a real nice guy.

The gateman writes a number on the guard station grease board, opens the gates and a brown UPS van rolls in.

The UPS guy hands me a package. A small package. And I sign it off.

I carry it back up to the house and Michael is there. Waitin.

'Oh Lamar, this is just so exciting!'

'Sure,' I say.

Michael rips through brown paper and then there's a box. It says 'Nike Air' on it in big blue type. His hands are shakin so bad that I have to open the goddamn box for him.

Inside there's a dead hamster with a golf tee affixed to its forehead with four sections of silver duct tape. The kid's eyes fill with tears. He slips his arm into mine.

'This is even better than I expected, Lamar,' he sobs. 'It's simply... magical.'

Chris

He'd never felt right. With his brown hair going grey and his broken heart. And when he thought about her, he knew there was nothing he could do.

None of them can say his name. On site they call him Consonant Chris. He's from the Ukraine and he's alone.

Consonant Chris 'phones his wife twice a week. It's been three years since he held her in his arms and kissed her beautiful face.

'Say my name,' he begs. 'Say my name.'

Broken hearts are never really mended and it's never really right.

Uri???

'Well listen, Uri, I want to do some talking now. Can I ask you a sort of personal question?'

'Go ahead, Michael. I can't promise that I'll answer it, but you can ask it.'

Michael looked at Uri then looked quickly away.

Michael picked up a biscuit, broke it neatly in half and laid the halves back on the plate.

There was a short silence.

'Forget it, Uri.'

'Michael. Listen, what's bothering you? Tell me.'

Michael picked up another biscuit.

'Uri, how long do things take?'

'What kind of things, Michael?'

'All things. Everything. Only my mother told me…'

'Your mother? What did she say?'

Michael carefully replaced the biscuit on the plate. He looked at Uri wildly.

'What did she say, Michael? What did your mother say?'

'She told me I'd broken my leg... Anyway how's your beard, Uri, I hear you've got a new electeric razor? They tell me, they tell me you plug it in wherever you go.'

'Electric, Michael, electric.'

Michael picked up another biscuit. His eyes rolled back in his head.

'Uri. Does my unnaturally short neck bother you?'

'No, Michael.'

'So you do think it's unnaturally short?'

'Yes. I mean no. It's a nice neck if you like that sort of thing.'

'What sort of thing, Uri?'

There was a short silence filled only with the muted hum of the Frigidaire and the angry buzzing of Uri's electric razor.

'Help me, Uri. Help me.'

'Of course, Michael. Troubles may just grow if they are locked away. How can I help?'

Michael picked up a biscuit and attempted to break it in half. It would not snap. He placed it on the floor and tried to grind it under his heel. The biscuit would not break. Michael kicked it away under the table in disgust. His eyes grew a shade darker.

'My neck.'

'Michael. High-necked clothes aren't "out" for you if you keep them neat and simple. This means avoiding chunky roll-top collars, broad built-up lapels or high-buttoned shirt collar necklines. You'll look good, Michael, in the new collarless shirts and neat Peter Pan collars provided they are not too tightly buttoned.'

'Oh Uri, that's wonderful. I simply adore Peter Pan!'

'I know you do, Michael.'

Gold

Michael leaned on the rail of the Klondike River Queen watching white wood smoke pouring from her twin black stacks. The leaden waters of the Yukon hissed past.

The arctic spring had given way to summer and he was going home. The air was heavy with balm of Gilead. Moosebirds and chicken hawks turned in the hard blue sky above and the banks of the river blazed crimson with fireweed and yellow with arnicas.

Below decks there was gold in suitcases and canvas bags, gold in bottles, gold in empty jars and food cans, gold in unwritten songs and unshed tears.

The little boat rounded a broad curve in the river and passed a rocky bluff. A cabin built of square cut logs hove into view. Beyond neatly cultivated vegetable plots, a lawned apple orchard swept down to the water's edge.

The sun slanted down the long slope of the lawn and settled in a crab-apple tree. The sour little apples were changing colour. Looking at them, Michael felt a sudden wild restlessness.

'I could do that,' he thought.

Tallest man

On the first day of our summer holiday we decided to go out early with the dogs and explore the labyrinth of twisting narrow lanes that connected our rented cottage to the nearest village. When we finally found it, the village was a real let down. It was shabby, dirty and deserted, the only shop was shut and the dilapidated pub was boarded up. We stood in disappointed silence surveying the scene and wondering what to do next.

The dogs heard it first, a faint cry which became a shrill grating squeal, building slowly into a full-blown shriek. Whatever it was, this tortured shrieking thing, it was headed our way and its cries of pain grew louder and more disconcerting by the minute.

A giant of a man rounded the bend in the lane

which became the main street. He was very fat and he was very tall. He wore scuffed black gumboots, grey mud-spattered trousers and a mustard cable-knit jumper with a red fabric patch on the front which in turn had been patched with a piece of green leather. The man was pushing an overflowing barrow of hay and by now the noise had become almost unbearable. The man flashed us a broad smile and we instantly saw that his teeth were an exact match for his jumper. He put down his barrow. The noise stopped.

'A very good morning to you both,' he said shaking our hands firmly, and then he dropped down on one knee to make a fuss of the dogs.

'Michael's the name,' he said. 'And I'm the tallest man in the village. That's my field over there by the pub and that's my shed that's in my field and that's my horse that's in it.'

Michael whistled through his mustard-coloured teeth, a hollow disembodied call which seemed to come from nowhere, and a horse appeared at the shed door. Michael whistled again, a dry, high-pitched note this time, and the horse, a roan mare with a gentle look in her eyes, trotted up to him and nuzzled his huge hand.

'Pretty little thing isn't she?' he said. 'Got her well-trained so I have. And not a nasty bone in her body.'

Our early morning walks became part of our holiday ritual and meeting Michael and the horse became our favourite part of it. We saw him every morning, tending to the mare, mucking out her shed, or sometimes just leaning on his gate, taking the air and admiring his domain.

There was something about Michael; he had a way to him, a magnetism. The dogs picked up on it instantly, and although we knew next to nothing about Michael we began to think of him as a sort of a friend.

The weather was perfect the whole week and our holiday was over all too soon. On our last morning we packed first, so we could enjoy the rest of the day without having to think about it, and so we ended up setting out an hour later than usual.

The August sun blazed high above the horizon and fields of ripe wheat stretched as far as the eye could see. The banked hedgerows hummed with insects and the verges sparkled with dog rose, foxglove and wild honeysuckle. It was a beautiful morning and the prospect of returning to the city filled us both with unspoken, formless dread.

We heard Michael long before we saw him, cursing and bellowing out the foulest language either of us had ever heard. As we rounded the gentle curve where the lane became the main street of the village,

Michael came into view. He had the horse pressed hard against the side wall of the shed, his huge hands clamped around her neck.

The horse was breathing hard and so was Michael. The mare looked terrified, the whites of her eyes showing and her ears clamped tight along her head.

Michael greeted us off-handedly as we drew level with his gate and then turned his attention back to the horse. He tightened his grasp around her neck and stared deep into her frightened eyes.

'Not so funny now are you, you fucker?' he said.

We returned to the cottage and silently packed our belongings into the car, wondering what the horse had done.

Deliveries

The Broad raps on the plexi-glass panel of the gatehouse, my home for the last ten days. Not ideal, but there's a couch and a TV, a microwave and a kettle and I'm allowed to a use a bathroom in the main house. It's been real quiet, no visitors. Just deliveries, lots of deliveries.

I let the Broad in.

'Nice place you got here, Lamar,' she grins. I catch a whiff of her lemon perfume and realise I probably don't smell too good

'Sure ma'am,' I say. 'Compact. Bijou even.'

'Come with me, Lamar,' she says. 'Walk this way.'

We follow a windin brick path edged with exotic flowers and neatly cut shrubs. It skirts around the floral clock and then crosses the amusement park.

After ten minutes or so we're in the woods which border the property on the southern side. We come to a clearin, a real nice secluded spot right on the edge of the estate. There's a pretty brook babblin, the birds are singin in the trees and centre stage there's a log cabin with a wisp of grey smoke at its chimney.

'So what do you think?' the Broad asks

'Huh?'

'What to do you think to your cabin?'

'Spiders,' I say.

'Spiders?'

'Spiders,' I say again. 'Hundreds of 'em. Stayed in one of these cabins with Elvis once. Spiders, hundreds of the bastards.'

'Not in this one, Lamar,' she smiles. 'Let's take a look inside.'

So we do. And the Broad shows me around, and boy, it ain't nothin like I've ever seen before. Sheetrock walls, electric lights, colour TV, fancy couches, drapes, antique furniture, fully fitted kitchen and boy oh boy, a waterbed.

'We had that reinforced, Lamar. I mean the bed. So you won't drown.'

'Look, lady, you got a problem with my weight or you got anythin to say pertainin to my personal appearance, you just let me know.'

The Broad just smiles at me. She has a nice smile the Broad.

'How about we checkout the kitchen, Lamar, and I fix you a coffee?'

'Lady, with the greatest of respect, no fuckin way am I ever drinkin your coffee ever again. How 'bout you show me the kitchen and *I* fix *you* a coffee?'

We push through double swing doors into the kitchen. Red enamel units, black & white chequerboard linoleum floor, chromed table and chairs and a real cool countertop juke box; a proper 50's diner in miniature. It makes me think of Elvis.

There's a woman at the sink. It's Mary! My Mary!

She's wearin one of them plastic aprons that make it look like you're nude.

'How 'bout you both stay out of my way, take a seat, and I fix you both a coffee?' she says.

'Mary?'

'Sure is, Lamar. How you been?'

'Good,' I say. 'No, I mean crap. Missed you, darlin.'

I take her in my arms.

'Marry me, my Mary,' I say.

'We already are, you big dumb lunk,' she says, and then she punches me full in the face.

Playful like.

Sherry

The room had a soporific warmth, an enervating deficiency of oxygen. But Michael and Uri, as usual, exhibited a controlled vitality unaffected by such external circumstances.

Wearing the white jacket of the healing professions, Uri came back from the cocktail cabinet carrying a brimming glass in each hand. He set one of the glasses down carefully on the low table beside his guest's chair.

'Your sherry,' he said with a smile, notwithstanding the fact that only a few sentences ago it had been a cocktail.

Lisa

He grabbed my hand. And he almost dragged me back to the sleeping bags that were opened now and arranged in a big circle around the fire.

I couldn't believe my eyes – each one had a couple in it and you could see bare arms and ankles in the flickering light. The kids were barely dressed!!! And what they were doing?? It was all Lego.

So this was a Lego bag Jag?

'Dear God,' I thought. 'Why did I ever come?' All I could hear was squealing and kids ramming nine-blocks where six-blocks should go. I wanted to cover up my eyes so as not to see what they were doing and cover my ears so as not to hear the heart-wrecking grate of non-compatible injection-moulded plastic.

Michael's hands were all over me. When his cold

hands touched my skin, something inside of me just snapped.

'No, Michael,' I cried. 'I don't want to!'

He put one hand across my mouth.

'Listen, Lisa,' he breathed like a husky little girl. 'You're going to put together a 1/32 scale model of Mac & Mike's water forts whether you want to or not! Culkin couldn't make that model and now we are going to! Don't fight me baby, I've got a wicked temper and you are liable to get hurt.'

I twisted and turned and tried to free myself. Michael laughed drunkenly in my ear.

'Have some more Jesus Juice, baby, and we'll put it all together.'

I had to do something to get away. My hand clawed at the Lego alongside the sleeping bag and suddenly I remembered something I'd seen in a movie. I grabbed a handful and flung it in his face.

Lucky

Michael sauntered down the drive towards Neverland Ranch whistling quietly to himself. He smiled as his beautiful house came into view.

It was a fine evening, the light was fading and the house looked wonderful illuminated in the soft semi-darkness.

Michael had passed a pleasant early evening with some like-minded chums: two hours of intensive Philately, just as he did every 2nd and 4th Tuesday of the month at the Los Olivos Church of Christ Community Activities Centre All-Purpose Room.

As he approached the house the front door swung slowly open and Lisa appeared framed in the doorway, the light from the hallway chandelier bathing her in its lustrous crystal glow. She looked stunning.

Michael laid his musket by the door and pulled her close. She melted into his arms; they kissed, and then went inside.

The maid brought in a plate of biscuits, a can of Jesus Juice for Michael, and quadruple vodka with a cherry in it for Lisa. They settled themselves on the couch and prepared to open the mail. It was their daily ritual.

'I already opened one from the bank, honey,' Lisa said softly. 'It was addressed to both of us and it kinda looked important.'

'Yeah?' Michael asked, his carefully plucked eyebrows arching up in question. 'What did it say?'

'Tell me about your evening first honey. How was Stamp Club?'

'The first rule of Stamp Club is that nobody talks about Stamp Club.' Michael said curtly. 'I've told you that before, Lisa. Now what did it say in the letter?'

'Can't you tell me anything about your evening, honey? Not specifics, just stuff in general? I'm sure you said something about perforations, or was it watermarks this week?'

'It was watermarks, Lisa, perforations are next week!' Michael snapped. 'Now tell me what was in the letter, Lisa.'

'Oh please, Michael, tell me a little about watermarks first, darling.'

'OK, Lisa, if you really want... In philately the watermark is a key feature of the stamp, and often constitutes the difference between a common and a rare stamp. The "classic" stamp watermark is a small crown or other national symbol, appearing either once on each stamp or in a continuous pattern. Watermarks were nearly universal on stamps in the 19th and early 20th centuries, but have generally fallen out of use and are not commonly used on modern issues. Some types of embossing, such as that used to make the "cross on oval" design on early stamps of Switzerland, resemble a watermark in that the paper is thinner, but can be distinguished by having sharper edges than is usual for a normal watermark. Now please tell me what was in the letter. What did it say in the letter from the bank?'

'Gee, Michael, that's just fascinating info about the watermarks, honey, maybe you could tell me just a little something about perforation?'

'OK, Lisa, just a little... In the early years, from 1840 to the 1850s, all stamps were imperforate, and had to be cut from the sheet with scissors or knife. Once reliable separation equipment became available, nations switched rapidly.

'In 1848, Henry Archer patented a "stroke process"

for the perforation of stamps, and in 1854 a "rotary process" was patented by William Bemrose and Henry Howe Bemrose. The common aspect of the two processes was the use of rows of small round pins to punch out the holes. The processes have been refined since then, but these are basically still the ones in use in the 21st century. The letter, Lisa. The letter. What did it say in the letter?'

'You know, Michael, I think I should begin by telling you that we have reached the end of a chapter in our lives and that we should both try to see that as being a good thing.'

'What chapter? What chapter have we come to the end of, Lisa?'

Michael sprang from the sofa and began pacing up and down the room in big striding steps, chewing at his moustache.

'What chapter? What chapter have we come to the end of, Lisa?'

'The chapter entitled *rich*, Michael.'

'What?'

'The bank has suspended payment, Michael. They're busted, we're busted. For the first time in our entire lives we're penniless. Isn't it wonderful?'

'What?'

'It means that we can live like common people and do whatever common people do.'

'But I don't want to live like common people and... What are you talking about, Lisa?'

'Don't you remember that it says in the gospel that whatever we do for Him will be rewarded with life everlasting? Well, for the first time in our lives we are truly rich... We are lucky to have each other and we have the children and we can never be poor and for that we are lucky.'

'We don't have any children, Lisa.'

'OK. But we have each other and we can never be poor and for that we are lucky.'

Michael strode over to the fireplace where a rack of hand-crafted American heritage fireside tools sat prettily upon the hearth. After a moment's deliberation, he selected the poker. The weight of it felt good in his frail hand.

'You are lucky, Lisa,' he said quietly. 'You are lucky that I do not kill you here and now with this finely-crafted example of American fireside history.'

Michael replaced the poker in the rack and walked out of the room, closing the door carefully behind him.

Lisa heard his footsteps and then his laughter echoing in the hallway.

She smiled to herself at this, because Lisa knew that after you have once laughed, you aren't really angry any more.

Now she's gone

I'm fine during the day and I'm OK in the evenings, but when I lie in our bed at night and everything's turned off I am frightened.

The police have been round three times. They say they have to ask me questions if a person dies at home.

I can be a cruel bastard at times. I didn't love her anymore but I still respected her, or at least I told myself I did.

It cost me three pound fifty for the death certificate. Three pound fifty. The test results came back today from the hospital, two days after the funeral. They say she's clear. I sent her out in the rain.

When they put her on the oxygen, the man told me I shouldn't smoke in the front room, as it was inflammable and there might be an explosion. I told him that 'inflammable' meant something else and that the word he was needing was 'flammable'.

I sent her out in the rain.

Biology

The phone rings and I pick up.

'Well hello...'

'Hello?' I say back.

And then some toffee-nosed British pansy starts asking me a whole lot of questions about marine biology.

'Who the fuck is this please?' I ask polite but to the point like. And then there's a girlish giggle.

It's Mike, and I figure however much I want to hurt him, Mike's still the boss, so I got no choice but to play along with the kid.

'Good morning, Lamar, and how are you this fine and sunny morning?'

'OK, boss,' I say. 'Super. I was abed with my Mary. We were just about to make—'

'Oh please no, Lamar! Oh Lord have mercy,

please don't tell me! How utterly repellent! The cold grey Antarctic sands, the waves, the spume, the seabirds whirling around, and all the time the underlying tragedy of the icecap melting. And the thought of you and Mary "doing it" like a pair of rutting walri... That's plural for walruses don'tcha know, Lamar?'

'Yeah, I did know that, boss. We were havin a cuddle, Mike, and we were just about to make breakfast actually.'

'Lamar, if you'd be so good as to come up to the main house there's some people here whom I'd like you to meet.'

So I pull on my mauve nylon slacks, splash on the Aqua Manda and ease into my yellow hide sports coat. I check myself in the bathroom mirror. Lookin tired, lookin old Lamar, and in bad need of a shave, I think. But still 250lbs of fine-lookin *hombre*.

I give my Mary a peck on the cheek before I leave.

'See you later, lardass,' she says, then punches the top of my arm so hard my fingers tingle.

'Ouch!!'

'What's up, pigface?' she says. 'It was only a love-tap,' and then she dead legs me. I fall back against the kitchen counter. And as I do, she kicks my left ankle away and I hit the very cold and very fancy linoleum.

I pick myself up and dust myself down.

My Mary just smiles.

'You clumsy fat motherfucker,' she beams.

I wipe the blood offa my face and I smile back.

'Don't be forgettin your hat now,' she says and skims it at me. The brim catches me in the throat and I stagger towards the door.

We are so much in love and I am so very happy.

I limp down the path edged with exotic flowers and neatly cut shrubs. When I come up to the house I let myself in and Mike's standin there in the hallway. He's wearing ridin boots this mornin, white silk jodhpurs a red huntin jacket and a black horse-ridin hat. There's a ridin crop jammed under his left arm. He looks excited.

'What's up, old chap, and what's with the limp and the shiner?' He chortles. 'Did you get tipsy and knock off a peeler's helmet?'

'I slipped in the shower, Mike.'

'Oh really?'

I look the kid in the eyes, beggin him not to ask me any more. It's then that I notice the monocle.

'Now what is that you want, Mike?'

'Follow me, Lamar,' he says.

On the ground floor of the house there's a wood-panelled trophy room where Mike's awards are exhibited in mahogany-framed plexi-glass display cases. Mike shows me in with a flourish even though I've been in that damn room a hundred times.

In pride of place there's a marble-topped Louis Quatorze dressoir, which is French for a Louis the 14th sideboard, which has a six-foot-long diorama of Snow White and the seven dwarves on it. It's in 1/32 scale, in glorious techni-colored wax; Snow White and the seven little fuckers frolickin amidst dyed lichen, fake grass, glitter, styrofoam rocks, plastic trees and such. And it is possibly the tackiest piece of *merde* you've ever laid *les oeufs* upon.

Anyway, to cut it short, this mornin the fuckin thing is gone. *Disparu.* And in its place there's a six-foot long aquarium bubblin away with gallons of water and galleons and sand and rocks and wavin weeds. And no fish. Just two big white snails stuck to the glass at the front on the inside of the tank. *L'escargot,* if you will.

'Nice snails, Mike,' I say.

'Shellfish, Lamar. Whelks to be precise. Nice, aren't they?'

'Sure,' I say. 'Nice whelks, Mike.'

'Have a seat, old boy,' Mike says, motionin me towards a real tasteful rococo white and gold throne which faces the tank. 'And it's *yeux* by way, Lamar. *Oeufs* are eggs; *yeux* is the French for eyes.'

'So you heard me back there describin your trophy room to the reader?'

'Yes I did, Lamar, but it's fine honestly. Don't worry about it.'

Mike pulls up a matchin white and gold rococo throne and sits at the side of me facin the tank. He lays his ridin crop across his knees and folds his delicate white hands in his lap.

So we sit there for a while, me and Mike and it's kinda peaceful listenin to the bubbles, watchin the soft green weeds wavin in the current and concentratin on the whelks inchin their way across the glass.

After a couple hours I really am hungry.

'Hey Mike,' I say. 'I really should be gettin back. I ain't eaten breakfast yet.'

Harold

Typical old guy. Half-suit. Smart jacket, Winfield jeans, turned-down gumboots. Hard hat, chained Parkies.

He were mumping and moaning all morning. Complaining about a pain in his foot.

Lunchtime, he sat on the steps of the snap cabin. Took his boots off. Dessert spoon fell out of the right one.

'You alright now, Harold?' we asked.

'Fucking spoon,' he said.

Uri????

'Well listen, Uri, I want to do some talking now. Can I ask you a sort of personal question?'
 'Go ahead, Michael.'

Michael picked up a biscuit, broke it neatly in half and laid the halves back on the plate.
 His eyes grew a shade darker.
 'Uri, how many people have died?'
 'What kind of a question is that, Michael?'
 'Sorry, Uri, that's not the question I meant to ask.'
 Michael looked at Uri then looked quickly away.

There was a short silence, filled only by the muted hum of the Frigidaire.
 'Forget it, Uri.'
 'Michael. Tell me.'

Michael picked up another biscuit, broke it neatly in half and wedged the halves into his tight-curled hair.

'Meeska, Mooska. Mickey Mouse.'

'Yes, Michael.'

'Uri, I'm thirty-five now and my mother said —'

'Your mother? What did she say?'

Michael picked up another biscuit and broke it. The biscuit shattered, spraying Uri with crumbs.

'What did she say, Michael? What did your mother say?'

'She told me that my mascara looks either sparse or sticky.'

'Well mothers don't know everything, Michael. Try using hot water instead of tepid water when appalling, sorry I mean *applying* cake mascara.'

'But you said to use tepid and not hot water. I'd like to flutter a pair of silky soft eyelashes at every girl I meet. You're giving me conflicting advice here, Uri, that's not what I pay you for.'

Michael picked up another biscuit and broke it neatly in half. He handed the pieces to Uri.

His eyes grew a shade darker.

Uri placed the halves on his left palm, passed his right hand over them and the biscuit was

whole once more. He handed it back to Michael.
There was a short silence.
Michael laid the biscuit back on the plate.

'No, Michael. That was earlier when we were discussing egg shampoo.'
'Anyway how's your beard, Uri? I hear you've got a new electeric razor? They tell me, they tell me you plug it in wherever you go.'
'Electric. Electric.'

Michael picked up another biscuit, broke it neatly in half and laid the halves back on the plate.
His eyes grew a shade darker.
'Michael, when applying cake mascara the trick is to use hot water rather than cold water. Don't be afraid to be lavish. Coat the brush with mascara; apply three fairly heavy coats on the tops of the lashes, then the undersides. At this stage the result will be heavier than you wanted. Now dip the brush into very hot water and brush lightly over the lashes. This way you'll set the mascara to make it last.'
Michael ran his hands through his hair. He looked at Uri wildly.

'Well listen Uri I want to do some talking now. Can I ask you a sort of personal question?'

Michael picked up a biscuit; Uri snatched it from him and threw it on the floor.

'Ask it, you weak-kneed wailer. Ask it.'

Michael picked up a biscuit, broke it neatly in half and flung the halves onto the floor. A maid came in with a wheelbarrow, dustpan and broom. She filled the barrow with broken biscuits and carted them off to the local orphanage.

Michael's eyes grew a shade darker.

'Uri.. Uri..'

'Yes?'

'Uri... No I can't.'

The maid returned with a fresh plate of bigger biscuits and a grateful handwritten message from the orphans.

'Uri.'

'Michael?'

'No I can't. I just can't...'

Michael tried to pick up a biscuit but he couldn't. His eyes grew a shade darker.

'OK, Uri... No I can't.'

'Yes you can.'

'OK, Uri... No, no, sorry. I can't.'

'For goodness' sake, Michael, just ask me the question.'

Michael picked up the plate, broke it neatly in half and laid the halves back on the table. His eyes grew a shade darker.

'Uri, I'm thirty-five now and my mother said—'

'Your mother? Mothers don't know everything you know. What did she say?'

Michael wrenched off a table leg and used it to batter the two halves of the plate into tiny pieces.

'What did she say Michael? What did your mother say?'

'She said you were in the woods with my dog.'

'But you haven't got a dog.'

'I know, Uri.'

'What else did your mother say about me, Michael?'

There was a short silence, filled only by the muted hum of the Frigidaire.

'Forget it, Uri.'

'Michael. Listen what's bothering you? Tell me.'

'Uri, Can I ask you a sort of personal question?'

'Go ahead, Michael. I can't promise that I'll answer it, but you can ask it.'

The maid came. She swept the room, removed the broken table, erected a folding picnic table, laid a plate of biscuits upon it and handed Michael a typewritten A4 sheet.

As Michael read her letter of carefully worded resignation his eyes grew a shade darker.

'Uri...?'

'An eyebrow pencil, sharpened to a point, makes an efficient eyeliner, Michael.'

'Oh Uri, that was simply... magical. You answered my question before I even asked it. How did you do that?'

'Because I'm a fucking psychic.'

There was a long silence, filled only by the muted hum of the Frigidaire and the angry buzzing of Uri's electric razor.

Katherine & Joseph

The phone rings as it always does when I figure I'm done for the day. And of course it's Mike.

'Quick question, Lamar.'

'Sure boss,' I say. 'Shoot.'

'So what did you think, Lamar?'

'To what, Boss? What did I think to what?'

'To my parents! Mary and Joseph? Sorry, Katherine and Joseph. What did you think?'

'I ain't never met your folks, Mike.'

'Yes you have, Lamar. You so have.'

'Gee I'm sorry, boss, I really don't recall, there's been a lot of introductions and new names and suchlike for me to be gettin a handle on since I started workin here.'

'Oh Lamar, for goodness sake! You are simply slaying me with your ridiculosity! It was only yesterday, can you please cast your mind back twenty-four hours? Anyway, you have a think and tell me tomorrow.'

And Mike puts down the receiver.

So I settle back on the couch, spark up a Hav-A-Tampa Jewel and I think back to what happened yesterday, the day my arm went numb, the day I developed a limp and a black eye, and the day I didn't get my breakfast till three in the goddamn afternoon. The day I spent a full two hours eyeballin a pair of whelks slidin across the glass in Mike's new aquarium.

And then I figure it out. Them two whelks were Mike's parents.

Goodbye

In the forest Michael convened a meeting with the three bears he'd shared a cave with all summer. They'd been good company, a little monosyllabic perhaps, but polite enough and fairly clean.

But they were always asking him questions.

Day after day they'd ask him questions. The same questions.

Who's been doing this, who's been doing that?
Who's been eating my breakfast?
Who's been sleeping in my bed?
Who's been stealing my paperclips, using my filing system, my carbon paper, my storage media?

When in truth they didn't have any breakfast, or any beds or any carbon paper, or office supplies, or really anything much of anything in the cave to steal or use, or to be asking him these constant 'who's been?' questions about.

Finally the constant questions got to be too much for Michael. He called a family meeting and sat the bears down around the kitchen table.

'So who's been calling a meeting in our cave then?' growled Poppa bear.

'And who's set the agenda for this meeting?' grunted Momma bear. 'And who's been using my duplicating machine to print out this agenda?' squeaked Grizzly junior.

'Enough with the questions already,' Michael said firmly. 'I've had a whole goddamn summer of this shit and I think it's time we laid down some ground rules. 'Rule one. When I ask you a question you answer it. You do not attempt to answer it with another question.'

'Really?' said the three bears in unison. 'And what's that supposed to mean?'

The bears were about to go to sleep for the winter anyway. One more great big feast of blueberry and salmon and they'd be out for the count till spring. The last thing they needed now was confrontation. They were sick of Michael anyway. And he knew it.

Michael seized his musket and flounced into the forest.

The communication trench that led from the cave to the forest floor was worn, and as baby bear reared up against a stump to scratch himself Michael seized his moment. Baby bear was tall for his age and it only took one shot. Baby bear crashed to the floor, still alive and breathing shallowly. Momma bear took him in her arms and Poppa bear threw his great arms around them both as they watched their child's life ebb slowly away.

'Why have you done this, Michael, why have you done this?' roared Poppa bear to the ashen trunks and the autumn winds.

'Enough of your fucking questions!' Michael roared back. And then he shot them both. One after the other.

Tito

I started playing guitar about a week after 9/11. I thought it might be a distraction from all the sadness the city was going through. Now I've been playing guitar for seven years. The time for me has gone by so quickly since that day. But I remember picking out my first notes and fingering my first chords that fall.

Off The Wall

I wake up with a start. It's two in the mornin and there's a storm outside. Which is good. A storm inside would be somethin else altogether. Then I hear a loud bangin. Also outside. I open up the cabin door and there's a boy on the step.

'What you want? You're on private property here boy, you better beat it,' I say.

The kid just stares at me, his soft brown eyes brimmin over with tears. 'It's me, Lamar,' he says. 'Don't you recognise me?'

And then I realise that the boy is Mike, soaked to the skin with no make-up on and his ass in his hands about somethin.

'Hey Mike, what's up?' I say, tryin to sound casual like.

'Oh Lamar,' he sobs. 'Something terrible has happened in the house.'

'Oh gee boss, I'm sorry. What?'

'Well you know the poster in my kitchen, the big one?'

'No not really, Mike, I'm sorry. And since when did you go in your kitchen anyways, Mike?'

'I go in there at the same time every night actually, Lamar!' the kid snaps.

'And why's that, Mike?'

'I go in there, Lamar, at about the same time every night, to look at the fucking poster.'

Well you could have knocked me down. I never heard Mike use the F word before. In fact, come to think of it, I never heard Mike use any kind of bad language before.

'Yeah, so anyway, this poster?'

'Butterflies of World War Two, Lamar. I got it from the museum. It was nine dollars, it came in a white cardboard tube with red plastic stoppers in both ends. They told me in the museum shop that the poster was A1 so I just had to have it, but when I got it home Lisa explained to me that saying a poster was A1 didn't mean it was a really good poster, it was just a way of describing the size, not saying it was a really good size either, just a way of saying that it was quite big, and then Lisa explained to me that it's the opposite way round to what you'd think and that even though you might think that if an A1 poster was quite big, then an A5 poster would be really big, in fact it's a lot smaller and that the only size bigger than A1 is not what you'd expect either and...'

'Yeah... anyway?'

'Well, it's fallen off the wall.'

'What were you using to keep it up with, Mike?'

'White tac.'

'Ah, well there's your problem, Mike! In environments with sharply changin temperature and humidity levels somethin such as white tac will simply not do the job long-term. It might hold for a while, but when the kitchen cools, at night for example, its adhesive properties will be significantly compromised.'

'Yes, but what are you going to do about it, Lamar?'

'What I suggest, boss, is that tomorrow I take the poster over to Mary's sisiter's, I mean sister's, art gallery in town and I get it framed up for you and then we can fix up the poster permanent like.'

'Oh Lamar, that's wonderful... simply magical. I never want that poster ever to fall off the wall again.'

Mike heads off into the dark and as I lock the cabin door it begins to sink in. He's black. Mike is black and I never knew.

Ice

As more and more boats drifted in with the ice, an air of panic began to settle over the Yukon Valley.

Michael existed on a strict macrobiotic diet that had made him quite thin and that made his face look even more sculpted.

In fact, a week or so earlier Michael had decided to bleach his scrotum with Benoquin, a bleaching cream prescribed to him many times over the years by his guitarist Dr. Arnie Klein.

He had never tried it before on his scrotum.

The cream burned and stung.

The ice itself was clear as crystal and slippery as glass. And navy blue in colour.

There is then a horrible story.

God

'Parents have been charged by God with the responsibility of guiding their children in the right paths... Don't you think, Lamar? It says so here in this book.'

'Sorry, boss?'

'Parents have been charged by God with the responsibility of guiding their children in the right paths. It says so here on page eighteen of this book, the new Machine Mart catalogue. It came through the letterbox this morning. It was slightly damaged, it looked like somebody might have dropped an iron on it.'

'Really?'

'Yes really. Incidentally, Lamar, the most likely protection from lightning is to install a metal post or pole a few feet from the house or property, extending several feet above the highest part of the building.'

'Er... Yeah, boss, sure.'

'Of course it is also true,' Mike says, 'that older folk move more slowly, don't you think? I mean you've seen me dance and you've seen my parents.'

'Your parents Mike? Ah yeah.. of course. Your parents.'

And then I stop feelin mad at him then. Poor kid, havin parents like that. So I ask him how they're doin, and if they like their tank, then he asks me about my parents and I can't find an answer for the kid.

For the life of me I can't remember them, their names, where we lived or any damned thing at all. And when I come to think about it I have no memory whatsoever of any single fact, or feelin or experience, or any fuckin thing that happened to me before I met Elvis.

I mean to say, I could write you a book of more than two dozen exemplifications wherein electricity clearly illustrates Christianity (with the words of Jesus written in red) but I could not tell you where I was born or if I had any brothers or sisters or anythin like that.

Elvis

When folks ask me about Elvis, I shoot 'em the same old line.

The job at Crown Electric, the record he made for his mom. Sam Philips, the Colonel, Graceland, Priscilla, Aloha from Hawaii, Bye-bye from the bathroom... the whole deal.

And ain't a word of it is true. Folks just got carried away. Elvis never existed. He never sung them songs, recorded them records, or waggled them hips.

It was all fake.

Bunch of us got together in a tavern one night and dreamed up the whole deal.

Folks wonder how come Elvis looked so different so many times. Truth is, we all used to take turns at bein him.

Sonny was Skinny Elvis, Red was Dreamy Elvis, I was Fat Elvis and poor little Marty got to be Dead Elvis.

Cheap As Chips

'Are you a good boy?' he would ask himself. Then he would answer, 'Yes you are a good boy.'

Michael walked around the house with his head wrapped in a vinegar-soaked cloth and frequently stood in the corner of the room. When his grandmother asked him why he was doing this, he said that he was preparing himself for the next episode of *Bargain Hunt*.

This was apparently the time when Michael began drinking rabbit's blood. He initially bought rabbits to cook and eat; now, more often than not he simply disembowelled them. He ate their flesh and drank their blood, convinced that this would turn his pale skin dark orange just like his hero.

One day, after some bad advice, Michael made an unwise investment and lost a lot of money on the limited edition souvenir thimble collection market.

'I'm going out,' he said. 'There's somebody I need to speak to.'

On the first day of December, Michael walked into the emergency room of the American River Hospital, Sacramento. He had a wild look. His clothes were filthy and he smelled bad.

'You better check my bedroom,' he told the doctors.

At the Psychiatric Unit, Michael's statements grew wilder and less coherent.

The police broke into his grandmother's house early one Saturday morning in late December.

Michael's grandmother lay dead on the kitchen floor, her mouth crammed with a collection of valueless limited edition souvenir thimbles, and a shattered rococo chair-leg jammed clean through her forehead.

The cops entered Michael's bedroom.

The Orange Duke bucked and reared against his shackles, his mouth bound with silver duct tape, his eyes gouged, his ears hacked away, and his dark tangerine face battered beyond all recognition.

Meadowhell

Michael took Uri's arm.

'We'll be safer like this,' he said. 'It's best if we keep together. It can sometimes get a little out of hand when I visit a Mall.'

Michael was right. As they entered The Meadowhall Shopping Retail Complex, Sheffield, England via the Debenhams entrance, an adoring circle of uniformed women quickly formed around the Israeli wonder man and a flushed nurse handed him a spoon.

Uri removed the spoon from its plush presentation case and bent it neatly in two using only the power of his mind. He handed the pieces of the spoon back to her.

The flushed nurse became very angry.

'That was my daughter's christening gift!' she

screamed. 'I wanted you to sign the box for me, not break the spoon in half, you wanker!'

The two boys executed a speedy exit and decided to head for Michael's favourite shop. No sooner had they entered Mothercare, than Uri and Michael were confronted by a group of aliens with big bug eyes and egg-shaped heads. Their leader handed Uri an extra-terrestrial spoon in a titanium presentation case. Uri signed the case carefully and handed it back. Their leader grunted, 'No, no!' and waggled his egg-shaped head. He thrust the case back at Uri and this time Uri removed the spoon from its titanium presentation case and broke it neatly in half using only the power of his mind. The veins stood out in the bug-eyed alien leader's egg-shaped head and he became very angry.

In broken English the bug-eyed alien leader with the egg shaped head grunted:

'No, no, no!! You insult us, earthling! The spoon was a gift from our people to yours, you wanker!'

By the time the two boys reached the Sheffield Heritage Shop where they sell the finest pewter, silver and steelware made in Sheffield, they were being tailed by a mob split pretty much 50/50 angry nurses/ angry aliens with big bug eyes and egg-shaped heads.

A security man emerged from the Heritage outlet. He was dressed as a buffer girl, a soiled brown paper apron barely concealing his big fake breasts.

'Stop right there thank you very much!' he bellowed. 'You're not coming in here! Sheffield is the home of cutlery and you are not welcome in our town, you wanker!'

Uri recoiled, deeply wounded by rejection and the repeated application to himself of the word 'wanker'. He turned away for a moment to regain his composure and pretended to be examining a window display of pewter tankards. When he'd had enough of them, he turned back to face the security buffer girl man guard.

Now Uri's eyes were wild and his face was drenched with sweat.

'No cutlery is safe from me!' he screamed. 'And when I scrunch my eyebrows, clocks and watches cease keeping time! My powers are for real and anyone one who says different is either deluding themselves or a very, very bad person!'

Uri turned stiffly to Michael.

'Take me to the Oasis food court now!' he bellowed. 'I tell you now, Michael. I tell you now, I'm going to beam myself onto the giant TV screen they have in there and I'm going to destroy the city!'

As the two boys closed in on the Oasis dining

area, steel shutters were dropping down in front of shop windows left, right and centre, and staff were being signed off early to allow them to spend their final moments at home with their loved ones. Sheffield had already been destroyed by a full-scale nuclear attack launched by local author Barry Hines in 1984, when he'd been refused extra scraps in a Walkley chip shop, and now it looked like a little case of history repeating itself all over again.

One by one the lights went out in Meadowhall. The 50/50 angry nurse/angry alien with big bug eyes and egg-shaped heads posse dwindled and fell away and soon the only sound to be heard was the two boys' own footsteps echoing along the avenues and alley ways of the huge deserted Mall.

But suddenly there were lights blazing up ahead. On the corner of The Arcade and High Street, one solitary shop was still open for business, defiantly retailing in the face of impending catastrophe.

None of the employees of The Kingdom of Leather had any friends or family to share their final moments with anyway, and as obedient minions of the Leather Lord they already considered themselves to be in a state of living death and so were afraid of nobody.

They swarmed out of the shop and seized Uri, dragging him kicking and screaming back to their upholstered leather lair.

They strapped Uri into a leather-faced executive chair and began to systematically mock him.

'I'm not who you think I am,' Uri whimpered. 'You've got the wrong Uri honestly.'

'Ooh are you then pal?' asked a morbidly obese pouffe salesman.

'I am *a* Uri.' Uri wept. 'That much is true. But I am not *Geller*. I am *Gagarin*, first man in space and it seems my whole life has gone steadily downhill since that glorious moment.'

Michael had entered The Kingdom of Leather by now of his own volition. Nobody had paid him any attention all afternoon and he was prepared to risk his life just to get some.

'So how come you can bend stuff, Uri, using only the power of your mind if you're not really him?' he asked.

'I can't bend stuff using only the power of my mind. Don't you understand, Michael?' Uri said desperately. 'I just bend stuff with my space pliers when nobody's looking.'

'Really?' Michael asked. 'Really? Oooh, you little liar!'

'Take him away!' barked a leather-faced executive. 'He's a wanker!'

'Goodbye Uri,' Michael said briskly, as the merciless leather folk wheeled his former friend off to the torture gardens of Leather Land. Then he picked up his musket and flounced off towards the reduced section.

It was quieter now, Uri's screams had subsided to a low animal hum and there were even a few late-night customers in the shop.

Michael sat alone on an overstuffed six-seater orange leather couch featuring a lattice-work base you could keep chickens in if you wanted to.

A woman came over. Her face was made of the same orange leather as the couch and her eyebrows were drawn on in the wrong place.

'You interested in this, love?' she asked Michael.

'It would be much nicer in yellow,' he said.

Moonwalk

His brothers leave the stage. So it's just him now, all on his own. The kid that all the fuss is about. And with his brothers gone he suddenly looks very small and the stage looks very big.

The spotlight finds him and his black sequined jacket sparkles in its artificial moonlight. He's wearin black penny loafers, white glitter socks, black trousers cut just above the ankle, a silver sequined shirt, and a single white glove on his left hand. He sets a black fedora on his head and strikes a pose.

Then he throws the hat aside with a flourish. The audience begin to scream. And then the music begins – his music. He starts to dance, just simple moves at first, then he spins and he jumps and he slides as the screamin builds to the howl of a taxiin 747.

I ain't never seen the kid in action before today

and it dawns on me that is the same funny little guy I catch pullin faces in the mirror or bustin into tears if a poster falls offa the wall at Neverland.

This kid is cool, this kid is sexy, this kid is dangerous. I ain't never seen anythin quite like this before, a guy so on top of his game, so effortless and so perfect and enjoyin every last goddamn second of it and nasty as you like.

And may God forgive me for sayin this, but he makes Elvis look like some fat guy dancin at a weddin.

He glides across the stage, except he don't seem to move, he goes forwards, backwards and nowhere all at the same time, and he spins faster and faster and faster until he finishes up on the points of his toes.

The music stops. I've been in some hysterical situations in my time let me tell ya, but this one beats 'em all.

My only real job tonight is to get the kid back down to his dressin room in one piece, so I do that for him, then I lock the door and stand guard outside. A guy comes runnin along the corridor towards me and I'm thinkin – *here we are, this is when it all starts* – but in fact he's a real polite young fella and he hands me a video cassette marked for Mike's immediate attention.

So I take it through to Mike.

'Stay and watch with me, Lamar,' he says.

We watch the show back on the VCR and I don't mind tellin you that I cried. I cried the whole goddamn way through.

When it's over he turns away from the screen and he looks me in the eye.

'Did I do OK, Lamar, did I do OK?'

I slip my arm around his shoulders and I fight the impulse to kiss the kid full on the mouth.

'You did great son,' I say.

'Unbelievable,

                    un

                        fuckin

                            believable.'

Anything

He was already one of the richest kids in the world. Anything he wanted, he just went out and bought it. It was a regular sight for him to be seen in an upper box surrounded by a gaggle of soubrettes drinking champagne at fifty dollars a quart.

Tan shoes and a dark blue suit. Not a good combo. And he's stopped ironing his hair.

His grandma is ninety-one years old. Her tired white hair is turning black, her worn-out teeth have regrown and she no longer needs her glasses in order to see. She has just been voted America's strongest woman for the third year running, and listed by the Southern Baptists as the author of one of the best five books in print for young people.

Perhaps you have noticed that the wires leading into your home or factory are covered with some kind of material know as insulation. Without insulation the wires would be dangerous for a person to touch.

It is really of no importance whatsoever to you to know that when a switch is thrown, one that connects electricity with your washing machine, the current starts flowing at the speed of one hundred-eighty-six thousand miles-per-second, through small coils arranged to create magnetism inside of the motor housing, which in turn, causes the armature to rotate at a terrific speed, turning other equipment that causes dirty clothes to become clean.

If you cut an orange in half and scrape out the fruit with a spoon you end up with a soft orange-peel cup. If you then pierce this cup at regular intervals, fill it with compost and plant a seedling tree in it, you will be able to trim the little tree's roots as they poke through the holes. This will hurt the little tree and stunt its growth.

Wisconsin

It's time to meet the fans. There's been a big group of 'em gathered outside the gates for almost a week now and every mornin I've been sendin the gateman down with coffee and donuts for 'em at Mike's request.

So, seein as Mike's got a new long-player scheduled for autumn release, he thinks it might be a good idea to shake hands, sign a few autographs, generate a bit of publicity and generally get his picture took with 'em.

Now the thing is that Mike is terrified of his fans. You wouldn't know it to see him with 'em, but he is absolutely shit-scared of 'em.

Don't get me wrong, he knows what they've done for him and he appreciates that they buy his records. He just don't feel comfortable around 'em.

I drive Mike down to the gates in his golf cart. This particular chilly but bright September mornin he's wearin a black jacket, a white on white tuxedo shirt, a tie with some sort of coat of arms embroidered on it, and a black knee-length skirt. He's also wearin a whole lot of makeup; even his damn hands are powdered. Mike's quiet in the cart, but as we approach the gates he begins his act, smilin and wavin and makin out that he's pleased to see his fans. He's a good kid really.

There's cheerin and clappin and shoutin and fifty pairs of hands thrust albums and 10x8s and pieces of paper through the bars of the gates for Mike to sign and there's an electrical storm of flashbulbs.

'Hwey Michwael,' yells a hare-lipped boy in the front row.

'Hey!' Mike yells back and gives him a high five.

'I love you Michael!' screams a girl with missin fingers and a lazy eye.

'I love you more!' he replies and then he takes her hand and kisses the stumps, at which point she faints clean away.

'URRGG MURRG,' groans a droolin girl in a wheelchair.

'And an Urga-doodledo to you,' says Mike. 'Nice wheels sister.'

As I scan the crowd I begin to realise somethin's

not quite right. One way or another they're all a bit spasticated. Every last one of 'em.

'Mike, what's wrong with these people?' I ask. 'I mean are they like a special part of your fan club?'

'No, not really, Lamar,' he smiles. 'They're just all from Wisconsin.'

Mike seems a lot more relaxed now and he's feelin confident enough to ask me to open the gates. The fans swarm in, crowd around Mike, have their pictures took with him and admire his skirt.

A man steps forward. A tall broad-shouldered guy; high cheekbones, square jaw, and a mane of golden hair.

'Howdy,' he says. He shakes my hand firmly, and right from the off I'm guessin that this guy ain't from Wisconsin.

'I've got notices up in the windows of my house,' he says. 'One says *Nature Garden*, but if you look at my garden its all weeds and rubbish. An I got a sign out front which says *The Dog Is No More. If it offends you don't look.*'

'Sure.' I say. 'Sure. Anyhow, what's your name, son?'

'Bob. Everyone calls me Loony Bob the Loon. But you must call me Lunatic Bob until we're better acquainted.'

'What do you do, Bob?'

'I'm a lunatic. Ask anybody, they'll all tell you the same thing.'

'Sure. Yeah Bob. But what do you do?'

'I sit in bars.'

'And then what, Bob?'

'I do drawings.'

'Drawins?'

'Yes, Lamar, drawings... in charcoal for preference and mostly depicting the scenes of senseless violence which occur late at night on the fringes of the Wisconsin Sheep & Wool Festival. You ever been to the Wisconsin Sheep & Wool Festival, Lamar?'

'No I haven't, Bob.'

'Me neither, Lamar.'

'How come you know my name, Bob?'

'I know all about you, Lamar. All about you.'

'Yeah? How come?' I ask.

There's a commotion as a gold Chrysler New Yorker limousine noses its way slowly through the crowd. The car stops just inside the gates and the Broad gets out.

'Bob!' she shouts. 'Get in the car now! You know you're not allowed out unsupervised! Get in the damn car now!'

Bob does as he's told and gets in without a word. I suddenly remember that I'm supposed to be head of security round these parts, so I marshal the fans offa the drive while the Broad executes a real slick three-pointer and turns the car around. The driver's window rolls down.

'Thank you, Lamar,' the Broad says.

'A pleasure as always ma'am,' I say and smile. And as the Broad smiles back, I catch a whiff of that great lemon scent.

Then the rear passenger window rolls down and I see Bob's face grinning like a skull, a light trickle of blood seepin from his left nostril and flecks of beige foam fizzin around the corners of his mouth. He tries to speak but it don't come out too clear, and as I lean in to catch what he's sayin, I notice that his wrists are cable-tied together.

'Meet the wife, Lamar,' he says through grindin teeth. 'Meet the wife.'

The Broad guns the engine, the rear wheels spin, then bite, and the limo speeds off down the drive, sprayin dirt, pain and gravel into the clear September air.

Elvis

I dreamt about Elvis again last night. I dreamt he modified my central heatin system without bein CORGI registered, and that he substituted a Honeywell three-way 22mm bore thermostatic valve, for a Honeywell 22mm bore three-way non-thermostatic valve, and that my ability to produce hot water/ heatin / hot water + heatin at will, was compromised beyond the realms of possibility.

Boy was I mad at him.

'Don't worry about it man,' he said. 'We've got a first aid demonstration on at club tonite with free splints, and then there's a band on... *Muscles Of The Heart*.'

Montana

Another day, another dollar. I ring the bell and Mike opens the front door. We musta lost the maid again; they never stick it for long.

'Morning, Lamar,' he chirps. 'Isn't it a beautiful morning?'

He's wearin a frilly orange shirt, tight white doeskin lederhosen and fluffy pink yeti boots. The outfit doesn't really suit him, the orange shirt and the pink boots. Well, what can I tell ya?

'Lookin good boss,' I say. 'Lookin real good.'

'Why thank you kindly, Lamar,' he smiles. 'I do my best. Now what can I do for you this fine morning?'

Seein as today it seems to have slipped the kid's mind that I work for him and not the other way around, and that he's also obviously in a great mood, I decide to ask Mike about the fans.

'Mike, you know them fans at the gate? The ones we spoke to yesterday? Well. They were all a little, how can I put this polite like?... They were errr... all a little fucked-up. If you don't mind me askin, boss, are all your fans that way?'

'Oh no, Lamar,' Mike says, 'those ones yesterday were fine... just typical god-fearing Wisconsin folks. There's a group from Montana, and you should see them... Golf injuries most of them actually. 'And his voice tails off like he might be thinking about golf.

'Golf is shit.' I say.

'Yeah...' the kid says thoughtfully. 'Golf carts are nice though.'

'Yeah, Mike, but golf is still shit.'

'OK, Lamar, I already agreed with you.'

'Say it with me, Mike,' I say. 'Say it with me that golf is shit.'

So we say it together and boy does it feel good.

'Yes anyway, Lamar, as I was saying, there's another lot of fans from Montana, and they really do break your heart, and the worst of it is, Lamar, that they expect me to heal them. They expect things from me which I really cannot give them. I mean, I can give them a hug and stuff but that's all really.'

'Sure, boss,' I say. 'Sure.'

'One time you know, Lamar, a woman had her

son brought to me on a stretcher. They laid the stretcher down on the ground in front of me, and drew back the blanket, and there was an ear. Just a single ear lying there on the pillow. His mother told me that the ear was all that was left of her son after his tricycle strayed onto a driving range.'

'Oh Sweet Jesus, Michael,' I say. 'Golf is so shit.'

'Yes I know, Lamar,' the kid says with no real feelin.

'So what happened Mike? To the ear I mean?'

'Well, I didn't want to hurt the woman's feelings, so I knelt by the pillow and whispered "I love you" into the ear.'

'Gee Boss, that must have been a magical moment.'

'Actually, Lamar, it was not,' the kid says all sniffy like. 'As I bent down and whispered those magical words, the words that every single human person yearns to hear, the woman began to scream and cry out in anger. She began beating on me and between the punches and the kicks and the tears and the abuse, she told me that her son was deaf.'

Smart Dave is Dead

He had a car. Which was a start. Austin Allegro Vanden Plas. Rexine seats, square steering wheel, shite gearbox fitted as new. I threw an apple core out of that car once. He backed it and he made me pick it up. I put it in the glove compartment for his mother. His mother dressed him. He rebelled just one time and bought himself a pair of driving gloves.

We'd always be in that car, rolling along to The Big Wheels of Motown, stoned, smacked, whatever. And anywhere was just fine by him, but only with the gloves on.

Same age as us, same face, same no chances. He got himself a job at Aldi. Echo biscuits, Kolumbo nuts, Goober grapes and Colway sauce. In his spare time he grew himself some man breasts.

'The chicks love 'em,' he said.

I'm a happily married man. I met this girl. Half Jewish, half Irish, bright and sexy as sin. I arranged to meet her in a pub. Set it all up. Dave said he'd drop me off.

'Give her one for me,' he said.

I never fucking went though, did I? Sat in another pub watching the clock and imagining where she was and wondering if she felt even half as bad as me.

He never did anything. He never smoked, he never drank, never even saw a needle.

And now Smart Dave is dead.

On The Wall

We've had a film crew in all week. And it's not been easy. For one thing, I've had to keep a real serious lid on the cussin, and for another, I've been tryin to keep Mike from loosin his cool on camera.

It's a British crew, you can tell that easy by their crooked teeth and their blotchy skin and the way all the women look like horses and the guys all talk like fags. And they're supposed to be doin 'a fly on the wall documentary' – or 'a fly *upon* the wall documentary'– as Pollyanna Toffington, their director, prefers to call it, but however realistic it's meant to be, they're always tryin to get us to do pretend stuff which they've dreamed up, because to be honest, there ain't a whole lotta real stuff goin on around here.

I mean, Mike's usually just up in his room with

his music and such, Lisa's attendin to her horses and I'm busy doin nothin all day.

So this particular morning, Pollyanna wafts into the lobby on a wave of plaque and body odour.

'Would you mind awfully, Lamar, if I had a bwief word in your shell like?' she asks.

'You fuckin what ma'am? Gee I'm sorry, I mean, come again?'

'Oh most amusing, Lamar,' she says. 'Perhaps we could have a quiet word. I have a suggestion to make.'

'Sure ma'am,' I say. 'Sure.'

So Pollyanna tells me what it is she has to say, and sure enough they've come up with another 'idea' that they think might be 'good to go' for me and the kid to act out.

The script is that Michael takes sick and I have to rush him to hospital and they get to film him in his Mickey Mouse pyjamas and it's all dramatic and suchlike, with flashin lights and medics and emergency rooms and the whole deal. So Pollyanna asks me if I'll run this brilliant idea past Mike, and asks if maybe Mike could add somethin to the piece 'to make it his own'.

So I climb the windin marble staircase right to the top of the house and I tap on Mike's bedroom door. A little voice says 'come in' and I do. Sure enough,

Mike's got his keyboards and drums and such out, and he's workin.

Mike peeps over the top of his toy piano.

'What?' he says.

'Er, Mike, Pollyanna asked...'

'What does that malodorous buck-toothed, horse-faced wench want with me this time?' Mike asks, a tad peevish like.

So I run Pollyanna's idea by him and he don't look none too struck by it.

'OK,' he says. 'If it'll get rid of them, I'll do it. I'll try to come up with something they can use and then maybe they can leave us be. Give me half an hour.' And then Mike's expression changes.

'Hold on just a cotton-pickin second, Lamar,' he says. 'I have an idea. Remember those fake blood bags Uri gave me?'

'Er, no, not really boss.'

'You know, the ones left over from that trick he played, when he miraculously removed his own appendix live on national television using only the power of his mind?'

'No boss.'

'Oh honestly, Lamar! Anyway, I have a plan, so you just take the lead from me OK?'

'Sure, boss,' I say.

So I go back down to the lobby and shoot the

breeze awhile with the unwashed talkin horse and her crew of British fags. Then I tell her that Mike's agreed to go along with her stupid plan. Except I don't say *stupid*, I say *interestin* and I don't say nothin about no fake blood.

Just then there's a knock at the front door and the maid shows a weird-lookin little guy into the hallway. The stranger's wearin a tie and a sweater and one of those all-of-a piece glasses, nose and moustache affairs you can purchase in any self-respectin novelty emporium. He's holdin a grip and there's a copy of the Watchtower tucked under his arm.

'Hi,' he says, 'I'm here to talk to you about God's word.'

'Would I be cowwect in assuming that's weally Michael?' Pollyanna whispers from behind her dirty unmanicured hand.

'Lady,' I say. 'You're smellin the same shit I'm steppin in. That's Mike fo sho.'

So Mike stands there in his own hallway pretendin to a be stranger and such, and his moustache is hangin offa his face and he's generally lookin less than cool.

'Today I'm here to talk to you about God's word,' he says. And then he becomes agitated, and commences clutchin at his chest.

'I have seen the end!' he screams. 'I have seen the

end! I have seen the end and not even the children were spared!'

And then he stops. And he squeezes his chest a few more times. Then he begins beatin on his chest like Tarzan of the fuckin Apes.

And nothin happens. So I'm guessin that the blood bags were supposed to go off when he was a screamin and a beatin on himself, but they ain't worked.

So Mike stands there awhile and then he pulls out all these books and pamphlets out of his bag.

'You should read these, Lardass,' he says to me, and then he turns to Pollyanna.

'You, my good woman, are from Englishland, I take it?'

Pollyanna shoots me a look.

'You'd better go along with it, lady,' I whisper.

'Yes I am,' she says. 'I am from England actually. How vewy perceptive of you.'

'And I also take it that you are too posh to wash?' the kid asks.

'I've been vewy busy wecently,' Pollyanna says sadly. 'And under a twemendous amount of stwess There have been swingeing job cuts at the BBC and I'm tewwibly afwaid if I don't deliver on this documentawy I may find myself on the scwap heap, especially as my last documentawy *Hewons Of The*

Wiver Twent did wather badly in the watings... But yes, you are cowwect. I have let myself go wather wecently, on the personal hygiene fwont.'

'Now get down on all fours and bark it out, bark it out,' Mike says sternly. 'Bark it out, I AM TOO POSH TOO WASH!'

And so, still hopin for her scenario, Pollyanna does as she's told. She gets down and she barks it out. When she's through, Pollyanna turns her face up towards Mike. There are tears in her eyes now.

'I weally need this job,' she sobs. 'My husband Tewence has wecently become wedundant so I am pwesently the only bweadwinner.'

'What did he do?' Mike who's not supposed to be Mike asks. 'What did your husband Terence do?'

'Tewence was a twee surgeon and a vewy good one too, but after he'd cut down every single twee in the London awea there was no weal need for his services any more.'

'Oh... that's so sad,' Mike says, a note of real concern in his voice.

'Now do it again. Bark it out again. And louder this time, much louder.'

Without warning, Polyanna rises up. And in one swift and beautiful movement, she spins on her heel and lamps him one, a sweet and righteous punch, a real haymaker, right between his eyes.

'Stitch that you little shit,' she says calmly. 'You are weally beginning to get on my thweepenny bits. You mess with me sunshine, you mess with the whole twailer park.'

Mike's flat out on the parquet now, a pool of real blood spreadin from his fake nose. Pollyanna calls her crew over and they begin filmin.

And I have to sympathise to a certain extent as I pack Mike into the 4x4 and drive him to the hospital.

Michael

Dear Mr. Mayor,
 I am a respectful citizen of your honourable town. Please send a helicopter to my house.
 My telephone number is 22337786456788456787 769872346567.

Continental

One minute I was in the lobby suckin on a Hav-A-Tampa Jewel pretendin that I owned the place, and the next I was wrestlin with some dumb kid on the newly lacquered parquet floor.

After a brief and kinda undignified scuffle, I stood the kid up against the finely grained pine panellin, drew back my fist and punched him full in the face. Which felt good.

'Welcome to Neverland Ranch,' I said. Witty like.

The kid was dressed kinda funny and smelled kinda funny so I'm guessin he may possibly have been French and just the thought of that made me feel real, real mad. So I decided to hit him again.

'Stitch that, Claude!' I yelled, strikin him upside the head and utterin a random French name. But I may easily have been mistaken. It could just as well have been Pierre, or Marcel, or even Philippe, or Giscard, or even some other fuckin French name.

Now, a smack in the mouth may be quite continental, but handguns are a guy's best friend, so after the break-in I decided to step up security a little.

'No guns in the house, Lamar. No guns.' Mike must have said it a thousand times. Lisa said it, the Broad said it, and I swear one time even the fuckin chimp said it.

'You want proper security, you need guns,' I told them over and over. 'You want me to head up security, you need to give me a fuckin gun.' I knew it. They knew it. I was serious as a hog shittin this time and I finally got my way.

I went downtown to check out what our local sportin goods emporium had to offer. The guy behind the counter showed me some real nice Italian 12 gauges and a beautiful 30.06 deer-huntin rifle.

'These guns,' I said. 'They're for shootin deer and bunny rabbits, Bambi and Thumper style of thing, right?'

'Yessir,' the guy said. 'That would be correct sir.'

'These are all fine guns,' I said. 'Each and every one of them. And really I'd like to take 'em all. Just the sight of a gun makes me feel big and hard and kinda pumped up, and sort of a helluva lot more manly, but what I need right now is a gun that's good for shootin people, so I'm thinkin maybe a handgun?'

'Yessir,' the guy said. 'That would be correct sir.'

We settled on a .38.

Zola

You might not think it, what with the way I look and the way I talk, and my penchant for violence regardin the French. But Emile Zola is the main man for me.

The way Zola describes a crowd is somethin else. You should read his books sometime. The Rougon-Macquart novels are swell, mostly translated from the French by a dude called Leonard Tancock, who must have had a real bad time in high school with a name like that.

Granny

He sits in his parlour as the night falls. It's just a night, but it's a big dark one.

After a while he lies down on his couch. Michael wants to sleep but the heat of the day has not given way to any cool of evening. Not this evening, and not any evening this poor kid is ever going to see. There's a scraping at the screen door. He unlatches it and there's an old lady standing there.

'Hi Michael,' she says. 'I'm your granny.'

He realises then, that he's naked, except for his black Bass Weejuns and a pair of sparkly white socks. Granny ignores his nakedness and they both go inside. Michael reclines lazily upon the couch whilst Granny busies herself in the kitchen.

He's confused by this, as Granny has been dead

for over two years. But as she doesn't mention it, for once in his life Michael decides to keep it shut.

He sits in his kitchen as the day breaks. It's just a day, but it's a big sunny one. Michael decides to do his laundry. He piles all his clothes into the washing machine, sniffs at what he's wearing, removes it, and puts that in as well. He keeps his shoes and his sparkly socks on.

Michael clicks the dial round to 60 and initiates the cycle. He wanders out into the sunlit yard and he's beginning to enjoy the sensation of the warm Californian air wafting around his body, so much so, in fact, that he decides that whenever possible, he will endeavour to avoid wearing clothes. They've always been trouble, he reflects, ever since he can remember.

Michael looks down at his abdomen. And he regards it with a swelling horror. He's still a young man, but there are ripples here and there, sections of flesh which should not be there, and which just hang down. Sections of meat, surplus to his requirements.

An older man would perhaps have referred to them as 'love handles' and 'man boobs' and tried to make a joke out of it all, or boasted about how the chicks loved them, but as Michael sees the beginnings of these unwelcome fleshy accessories developing on his torso, he panics and begins to chew furiously at the insides of his mouth.

His Granny ambles into the yard. She's wearing a thick wool coat in spite of the heat, and Michael realises that he is naked except for his black Bass Weejuns and a pair of sparkly white socks and that this is the second time that this has happened. Granny ignores his nakedness and they go inside. This is also the second time that this has happened.

Michael reclines lazily upon the couch. Granny puts down her grip and removes her coat. She opens the grip and extracts a selection of interlocking Tupperware containers.

'Nothing lasts for ever, Michael,' she says sadly. 'Except for Tupperware of course, and even that goes a bit yellow after a while.'

'I know, Granny, I know,' Michael says, as he fidgets about, trying to find a nice comfy position. He turns over onto his front.

Granny takes a ball-peen hammer from her grip and strikes Michael with it. She strikes very accurately and with surprising power just the once upside the back of his head. The rear of Michael's skull collapses inwards. The epidural haemorrhage accumulates rapidly. He takes less than two minutes to die.

Granny rolls Michael off the couch and onto the floor. She places her largest Tupperware container squarely under his neck, takes a folding pruning saw from her grip and begins sawing steadily at her dead grandson's throat. She tires, takes a break and tries again.

Eventually the head comes off.

Granny produces a long-handled sundae spoon from her grip. She goes in through the collar of the neck and fishes around inside the base of Michael's skull.

Granny finally makes contact with what she's here for, and scoops out the tiny metal capsule, which contains the microfilm.

Mods

Carolyn was sixteen and in her senior year of high school. Michael was eighteen and also a senior, but since Michael was older than Carolyn he was in fact senior to her. Michael had a job and a car, such as it was.

Carolyn was musical and spent her afternoons practising the piano. Carolyn and Michael began going steady soon after they became seniors and as their senior year wore on Michael and Carolyn found themselves spending more and more time together. It was the springtime of their relationship.

And then came that fateful evening.

Michael and Carolyn decided to go out for a drive in the forest. They were chatting amicably about nothing much when Michael glanced into the rear-view mirror and noticed that they were being tailed by a swarm of angry mods riding Vespas bedecked with mirrors and all manner of chrome twiddly bits. This came as no surprise to Michael, in fact he'd been expecting some kind of trouble because the previous weekend he and Carolyn had cornered several mods in the local graveyard and done them over goodstyle. Now the mods were out for revenge.

Michael waited for a clear spot at the side of the road and when he found one he pulled over. The mods pulled over behind them and dismounted.

Without speaking he and Carolyn walked around to the rear of the vehicle and opened the trunk. Carolyn armed herself with an iron bar and Michael selected a pickaxe handle.

And so the quarrel was on – the kind of quarrel that involves bitter words, stinging sarcasm, pickaxe handles and heavy iron bars.

Beards

Graduation provided many thrills and what with class functions, a class picnic and a banquet, Michael and Carolyn spent a great deal of time together. On class night the class prophecy was read and it was predicted that Michael and Carolyn would live happily ever after.

One Sunday morning after church, they decided to venture across the glacier. The ice was clear as glass and navy blue in colour.

Due to the storms which howled ceaselessly across it they were unable to pitch a tent and were compelled to sleep in the lee of Carolyn's cream heart-shaped vanity case. Their way was continually blocked by fissures, some of them obvious, some of them obscured by snow. These fissures forced them to take endless detours and the glare from the snow made them rub their eyes so vigorously that their lashes were scrubbed away.

Three months into the trip Michael and Carolyn were unrecognisable to each other, they had both lost a good deal of weight and their sallow faces were masked by unkempt foot-long beards.

By the fourth month Michael and Carolyn could no longer speak. They merely struggled across the ice for hours in silence, too tired to even grunt.

The only sound they could hear was keening of the gales and the distant laughter of the townsfolk.

Unlike Most Regular Guys

Unlike most regular guys, I enjoy the fortnightly supermart shop with my wife. She's a sport is my Mary and in a public retail environment we kinda like to kid around a little. So comin out of Wal-Mart, I grabbed the trolley off of her and said 'save your wrists for later chicken,' and patted her ass a couple times. She wouldn't let go of the trolley and we had a bit of play tussle for control of it, durin which her ass got felt a couple more times and I have to confess I had the makins of a semi goin on right there in the parking lot.

So I rubbed myself up against her so she could feel my new .38 in its shoulder holster pressin into her back. Mary let out a playful scream and I held her tight around the waist, her butt in my crotch. Boy was I feelin' stoked!

It was then that I saw Mary's reflection in the tinted glass window of a Ford pickup and realised that she was behind me and pushin our trolley.

The other broad was OK about it after I apologised.
Not great, but OK.

They

They told me to buy my gym-er-nasium cap straight away.

'Pamper yourself like a king,' they said

They all came round the house and they stood in the front yard shouting stuff out in funny high-pitched voices.

'Achieve picture perfect weight and enjoy your life now.' they squeaked.

'Increasing acceptance of this standard has given birth to a number of X,' they said.

A woman broke away from the pack. She teetered up to my front door on scuffed red stilettos and knelt.

'Everything is a cipher and of everything he is the theme and the new Machine Mart catalogue is out now!' she bellowed into the letterbox.

I was upstairs in an upstairs room, dashing away with a smoothing iron.

I opened an upstairs window in the upstairs room and dropped the iron with pleasing accuracy directly onto the back of her head.

Unicorn

Michael takes the box down from its special shelf in his bedroom, and lifts the lid. The unicorn is lying there.

Carefully, Michael cups it into his hand. He smoothes the silver tape down onto its forehead and strokes its soft brown fur.

Michael begins to sing.

This is my box
My box of great tastes
My box of touch
Of dreams and ambitions
My box is fashioned from sequins, diamonds and fluff
With icicles on the lid
And tiny whispers in the corner

The unicorn opens its eyes, stretches, and smiles up at him.

Bad

Awoke at 5 this a.m. and she was gone. I thought about puttin on a shirt and a tie and goin for a stroll, just to be different.

Instead, I sat on the edge of the bed in my shorts, sparked up a Hav-A-Tampa Jewel, and thought about my life and the way that it had turned out. And I felt OK. Mildly disappointed, but OK. Far, far, away in the woods I heard an owl shriekin a hysterical horror-flick scream. And as I sat there on the edge of the bed, a feelin of complete and unholy dread washed over me. I felt sure that somethin bad was going to happen today, to me, Mike, Mary or the Broad, or maybe to us all. I wasn't sure what, but I knew somethin was goin to happen and that when it did, it would be real, real bad.

And it turns out that I was right.

Klondike

September. Another year almost gone and still nothing to show for it. The Yukon valley on fire with colour. Aspens orange, buckbrush crimson purple. The leaves begin to fall and gradually the valley turns grey. The mornings grow cold and the pale sun loses its warmth. The days shorten.

In the forests the hare, the ptarmigan and the weasel turn white. The bears go back to sleep. The birds are long gone, only the juncos and snowbirds remain, ready to sit out the winter.

Along the margins of the Yukon cat ice begins to form.

The two boys poled up-river and beached their boat on gravel shoal at the mouth of a creek. They shouldered their heavy packs and set off, struggling through wet mosses and sucking black sand. The clear shallow water of the creek teemed with small fish and clouds of flying insects infested the sharp autumn air.

Uri turned to Michael. 'It's here somewhere, Michael,' he said. 'Somewhere close. My voices... my inner voices are trying to tell me... I'm getting some strong energy.'

'What's here, Uri?'

'The gold, Michael. The reason why we're here.'

'Uri, could you explain to me the difference between a male and a female horse? I know you did twice before, but I've forgotten again. I'm sorry.'

They continued in silence until they came to a fork in the creek.

'Look Uri, it's a fork; you like them don't you Uri? You like forks don't you?'

Michael began to giggle. A high-pitched, tittering snicker. Uri ignored him.

They took the left fork of the creek which by now had a muddy tinge.

'Someone's working upstream, the water's muddy!'

The two boys crept upstream, alert and silent. The narrow creek grew heavier and heavier with mud and then the water turned red. The two boys stopped when they saw that. Then they heard a commotion in the distance.

Up ahead there was a horse in the creek. A roan. A once fine animal. The horse's back and flanks were suppurated with sores, its thighs running with blood and its ribs protruding. Thrashing on its side in the water, the horse was nearly dead. Upstream from the horse the tethered bodies of a man, a woman and a little girl bobbed in the creek. Their wrists and ankles were tied and they were already dead.

Set back a little from the water's edge was tiny mud-roofed cabin.

The door hung open. A twelve by twelve-foot room without floor or windows. A rickety double bedstead and a sheet-iron stove. In the centre of the room a panning tank used to test the pay dirt.

And then Michael and Uri saw the gold. Accumulated in jars and bottles it glittered in the dim light of a guttering candle.

Near the stove there was a furry bear and a doll without a head.

Neat

Mike was down to his last box of Big Red Gum so he had me drive out to Los Olivos to stock up. Mary come along for the ride. On the way back to the ranch we passed a roadside chaffinch competition such as you often see in this part of the world in the fall.

Around two dozen cages hung from a fence, each one containin a finch previously blinded with hot needles. I explained to Mary that the winner of the contest would be the chaffinch who sung his little song the most times durin the course of an hour.

Behind each cage stood a Belgian nail-maker frantically urgin the chaffinches on, shoutin in Walloon for them to sing over and over again.

Mary asked me how come the birds were blinded.

'They're supposed to sing more if they can't see,' I told her. 'It's illegal to blind them these days, but folks still do it.'

And as I told her I imagined them doin it. The little bird grasped tightly in a fist and the hot needle searin its tiny black eyes.

'I think it's neat.' Mary said. 'I think it's really neat.'

Garden Birds of Britain

Me and the Broad are sat at the kitchen table in my new cabin.

We're drinkin coffee, made by me. Mary's visitin with her sister for a coupla days so I can use a little company. Me and the Broad chat about Mike for a while and then I show her my new wall chart, featurin 'Garden Birds of Britain', some of which are also garden birds of the US of A. Then she asks about my new gun, so I show her that as well.

Then the Broad stands up, moseys around the table and settles herself on my lap. As she cosies up to me I catch that great lemon scent and she slips her hand inside my shirt. She rakes her long nails across my chest. It feels wrong but I like it all the same.

'Moobs,' she whispers. 'You've got a lovely pair of man boobs, Lamar; I see 'em quiver sometimes and they make me crazy. How about we test out that new waterbed of yours?'

'But... but what about my Mary? What about Bob?'

'Your conscience is your concern, Lamar. And Bob? Well you've met him. He's a lunatic.'

'He sure is, ma'am.'

'So anyway whaddya say, Lamar? I've been hot for you ever since you punched that French kid and I know you like me.'

'So he was French, I goddam well knew it! I'm not sure, I mean I want to, but I'm sorry, ma'am, it's just a bit of a surprise. A nice surprise.'

'Look, Lamar,' she says, 'how about we get to know each other gradually. I pay attention to developing the charms of my personality, instead of allowing physical intimacies, reserving my friendship for you, my special young man, and then together we experience the true satisfaction of a wholesome courtship that culminates in marriage and us establishing a happy home together in which I and my husband share equally in the genuine pleasures of holy wedlock?

'Or shall we just fuck?'

So we do. And when it's over I slip on a robe and go back to the kitchen to fix us both another coffee.

While I'm waitin on the kettle to boil there's a flash and somethin hits me in the chest. Hard. I fall to my knees and realise I've been shot. I feel sick and I smell my blood. I hear the Broad screamin from the bedroom and then there's another shot and the screamin's replaced by the sound of runnin water. It's then I notice that the words 'ARE GAY' have been added to 'GARDEN BIRDS OF BRITAIN' in thick black marker pen. I recognise it as Mary's writin. Then I die.

Lard

Michael perched himself on the arm of an easy chair and smacked his lips over a glass of sweet sherry. His head was as round and bald as a yellowing bladder of lard. Chins concertinaed over his collar and in a thickly accented voice he told the sick man's wife to arrange for two men to go at night to the grave of a recently hanged man.

One man was to stand at the head of the grave and the other at the foot and for an hour they were to flourish their swords in the air while Michael stood by with a bottle of brandy and wrestled with the spirit. Then a sword was to be plunged into the middle of the grave.

The sick man was instructed to strap a freshly killed owl to his forehead and the wife was told to visit the house of the hanged man and make a pin case out of the straw she gathered there. Her husband was then to wear the pin case under one arm and a horseshoe under the other.

Michael charged the couple $20 for this ridiculous piece of advice. It was all the money they had in the house. They'd been collecting it in an old fruit jar hoping to amass enough to pay for a painful and totally unnecessary eye operation for their only child. Michael scooped up the coins, thrust them deep into the left hand pocket of his jodhpurs and strode out into the night laughing.

Cool

So the next thing I remember is that I wake up, and some joker's tryin to pull the weddin ring from offa my finger. I figure that I'm probably not technically married to my wife no more on account of havin recently been murdered by my wife, so I let whoever it is go ahead and take the damned thing while I try to figure a few things out.

I feel like I'm in a crib, like a child's cot, or a box or somethin, and it don't come as a deal of a surprise when I open my eyes to discover that it's a casket. And also, and on the plus side, they've got me done up in a real nice peach coloured two-piece suit, the sleeves of the jacket rolled up a tad. Classic yet contemporary like.

I hear a pair of heels clip-cloppin across a hard tiled floor and I then catch a whiff of lemon scent. So I know who it is. I close my eyes again.

'Oh... nice suit, Lamar,' the Broad says. 'Very nice. Classic yet contemporary.'

'Thank you kindly, ma'am,' I say and open just the one eye.

The Broad rears up on her hind legs. 'WEEHEE!!!!!!!!' she whinnies like Champion the fuckin Wonder Horse, and it's definitely the first time I've ever heard a dame make a noise like that, and I mean under any circumstances let me tell ya, and then I feel the casket shift a tad on its trestles as she clamps her hands down onto the edge of it to keep from fallin over.

Then the Broad throws back her head, and she laughs and laughs and laughs.

'I knew it,' she says. 'I knew it. After what you did before I thought you might just be able to do it again!'

'What did I do?' I say. 'What did I do before?'

'You know, Lamar, she says, 'when you slept? When you slept for sixteen years and never needed the toilet?'

She leans into the casket and slips her hand inside my shirt. She rakes her long nails across my chest and then places her hand upon my heart. It sure feels nice.

'As I suspected,' she says. 'No heartbeat.'

'My heart stopped beatin the day Elvis died,

ma'am,' I say. 'And it's been that way ever since.'

I notice now that her face is wet with tears and that she's regardin me more tenderly that my mother, my father or anybody in my whole life ever did.

'I think we should get you out of here now, Lamar,' she says. 'Quick as we can.'

'Do I get to keep the suit?'

'Yes, of course you do, my darling.'

'Now that's what I call cool.' I say.

Glass

There was glass and blood.

I went to touch him and he was dead.

I'd never touched him when he was alive and now I wish I had.

Sometimes I feel like I spend my whole life covering up Michael's mistakes.

Meanwhile Back at the Ranch

'So what about you?' I ask the Broad.

'What do you mean, what about me, Lamar?'

'I mean what happened to you?'

'Mary missed. She was so riled up after she'd defaced the wall chart and done with you, that she took a wild shot at me and missed me by a country mile. The bullet went through the mattress, through the base of the headboard and then right on out through the back wall of the cabin, but I took my chances and I played dead all the same.'

And then the Broad tells me the whole story. And it's the usual style of thing such as you might see in any daytime TV show. The cops, the medics, forensics, the whole works, and as she tells me the story it seems to me like my death was a real big deal, a much bigger deal in fact than my life had ever been.

So when the Broad gets to the part where they take my body away and she makes a statement downtown and then they put out an APB for Mary's arrest and they pick her up on a bird-table webcam disguised as a bird of prey hangin around and bitin the heads offa chaffinches and generally disturbin the peace of sleepy downtown suburban Los Olivos, the Broad tells me there's somethin else she needs to say, and the way its goin I'm expecting Lieutenant Columbo to pop up and say, '*Excuse me ma'am, just one more thing.*' But instead, she shares with me a detail which is so tender and which touches me so deeply, that it makes me realise just how very much in love with the Broad I am.

'And do you know,' she says. 'When I got back to the ranch early that evening I went down there again to your cabin, I don't know why, I just did. And out back I found a rabbit with a big ragged hole gaping in its pretty little head, it must have been frolicking happily behind the cabin one moment and then taken the bullet that was meant for me the next.

It was barely alive,' she says, her voice crackin with emotion. 'Lying on its side in a patch of dappled sunlight, twitching weakly beneath a neatly cut ornamental shrub. It was fighting for its poor little life, its soft fur all matted with dark blood, and I felt so sorry for it, and so grateful to it for taking the bullet which both Mary and the Lord Jesus had intended for me in my sinfulness, that I felt that I simply must do something for it to express my gratitude...' And her voice tails off like she's rememberin whatever it was she did to express her gratitude for the little bullet-takin bunny rabbit.

'So, so, what did you do?' I ask.

'I did what I had to do, Lamar,' she says. 'I did the decent thing. Something which many Americans would maybe have shied away from doing. I took two cinder blocks out from under the cabin and I laid the bunny on one and used the other to pound that little bunny's head until it was flat. It squeaked a bit to begin with, but that soon passed. I whacked the block down onto its skull over and over and over and over, until it was just a fine paste, until its skull was broken into thousands of tiny gritty, grainy little fragments. And then, Lamar, I crushed its poor little body too. I worked along it, methodically shattering every bone from neck to tail and I pulped it all right down too, just to make sure that the poor little darling wasn't suffering no more. And then I scraped up the bunny paste onto a spare cedar roof shingle which I also found under the cabin and tossed it into the woods for the chaffinches and owls and yellowhammers and greenfinches and crossbills and woodpeckers to feast upon. Did I do the right thing, Lamar? Did I do it right?'

'You did great, lady,' I say. 'And you remembered some of the birds from the wall chart too. You're a good girl, a real good girl.'

And as I picture the Broad pummellin the livin fuck out of that poor little injured bunny while namin some of the Garden Birds of Britain, I fall in love with her all over again.

One Morning

One morning while watching the television news on his television Michael had an idea.

A few days later Michael went to church.

During the meeting his body trembled violently and he began to wrestle with various pieces of furniture.

The following day Michael attended another meeting. Halfway through the sermon he switched on a transistor radio.

After that he wrestled some more furniture.

Shot

I'd always thought that when death came it would be the end, and that when it came, they called your number, you stopped doin whatever you were doin and you just fell off your perch and rotted on down.

But I'm OK, I'm fine. I feel maybe a tad more peevish in the mornins than I ever used to, but I'm happy enough in myself.

I had to go to the burial, I just had to. I mean anybody in my situation would have done the same. The temptation was just far too great.

I put on my new two-piece peach suit and rolled the sleeves down a tad, out of respect for whoever or whatever it was that the Broad had had put in my casket and hid myself behind a flashin blue neon sign which read *Sleepy Lawns Cemetery Welcomes Careless Drivers.*

Mike was there, dressed to the nines in a black silk suit and really lookin the part for once. The Broad was there too in a sexy tight black number, and there was quite a few other folk, wearin their Sunday clothes. Which was pleasin.

As they lowered my casket into my very own little piece of personal oblivion Mike cleared his throat like he had somethin important to say and everybody turned to look at him.

'You're fired, Lamar,' he blurted out.

And they all laughed and as they laughed he realised that they thought he was just being a wiseacre and he began to cry. And when they all saw him cryin and realised that he thought that they had laughed because he thought that they thought he was just being a wiseacre and that was what had made him cry then they all began to cry. And that made Mike cry more and so it made them all cry more.

And it all went on like that for about an hour. Which was fuckin excellent. And in its own way, it was a really sweet thing for the kid to have said. And it meant a lot to me.

As soon as the people had cleared out, I crept across the grass to check out my tombstone. *Former Elvis Bodyguard* it read, just like I always knew it would.

Now, as I strolled across the manicured lawns and skirted around the rose beds and neatly clipped shrubs I knew that this wasn't really happenin and that I really was dead and that all of this shit was just like one of those crappy stories you might read in a thin book written by some dumb English kid with a big nose and a funny surname. But it was a real nice day and I felt like takin the air for a spell anyway, just to get the scent of death from outa my lungs and nostrils. So I found myself a bench, lit up a Hav-A-Tampa Jewel and sat there drinkin in the brilliant bone-yard sunshine.

I took a long drag on the Hav-A-Tampa and nothin happened. I tried to inhale again with no success and it came to me just then that I wasn't breathin no more. Funny how little things like that can slip your mind sometimes. So I held onto the Hav-A-Tampa, let it burn down to about an inch and then placed it betwixt my thumb and forefinger and I thought about all the Hav-A-Tampas I'd ever smoked in my life and how today I didn't seem to be dead no more, and how Elvis smoked 'em too and I wondered if he was really dead or still out there somewhere, maybe just annoyin the golfin folk of Montana, and how I might get a message to him.

And then I flicked the Hav-A-Tampa away, flicked it clean away, way across the manicured lawns, the rose beds, the neatly clipped shrubs and towards the carefully crafted floral tributes.

There was a flash and a dull roar, as a whole gallery of carefully crafted artificial floral tributes for people who really were dead burst into hot red flame.

Seems like me and fire just can't get along these days.

So I decided to get the fuck away from there a.s.a.p. and made for the road.

Outside the Chapel Of Rest a gold Chrysler New Yorker limo with the motor tickin over shimmered in the late afternoon sunshine. As I approached it the passenger door swung open and the Broad leaned across from the driver's seat and gave me a smile.

'Get in,' she said.

She's got a real pretty smile, the Broad...

Metal

Michael sits up in front of the bedside mirror with a piece of metal in his head.

They've shaved his head and in an effort to save his voice they've amputated both his legs. One at the hip, one at the knee.

'Your dancin days are over, son,' the priest tells him.

He leans towards the priest.

'What's that round your neck,' he asks. 'That thing?'

'A crucifix, son. Proof that our Lord Jesus died for all us sinners.

You got faith 'n airthang?'

Michael snatches it from the priest's neck and swallows it whole.

'Fuck you father,' he says,

'Fuck you, fuck you, fuck you, fuck you.'

Smile

We go for a coffee, me and the Broad. And I mention about the breathin with particular reference to the *not being able to* part of the deal. The Broad says it don't matter and that I needed to quit smokin anyhow, apparently it ain't so good for your health these days.

'Let's find ourselves a sunset,' I say.

'There's one every day in America,' she says. And then I kiss her like I've never kissed anybody before and she kisses me back like I've never been kissed by anybody before.

And then we find ourselves one of America's famous daily sunsets and we drive into it.

She's got a real pretty smile, the Broad.

Strongest Man

Got a letter this mornin and how do you reckon it read?

Shockin pink envelope, glittery ink and rounded girlish handwritin with miniature hearts for dots above the i's and j's, so I knew straight off it was from Mike.

The dumb kid had written Par Avian on the envelope instead of Par Avion, so the letter had been delivered by bird and as a result was almost six months late.

> Neverland Ranch
> Monday
> Almost six months ago

Dear Lamar,
It has not escaped my attention that that you have died (in fact I attended your funeral and I like to

think that I lent a certain tone to the occasion in my own small way), but I still think of you fondly and since you have obviously forgotten to write to me, I have decided to drop you a line or two.

I have reached a great decision!!!!

I'm leaving Neverland!! In fact I'm leaving America for good. A business opportunity has arisen in Doncaster UK and after much deliberation Lisa and I have decided to take it.

A number of factors have influenced our decision, my records are not selling quite as well as they used to do and the house has become increasingly expensive to run.

I've had a growing sense for some time now that I am not welcome in America any more. For me, this was brought into sharp focus a couple of weeks ago when I when invited to attend a prestigious awards ceremony in order to collect a prize for being America's Strongest Man. I received the award (rather graciously I thought), made a little speech and in general created a simply magical evening. I was slightly puzzled that nobody asked me to pick up anything heavy or tear asunder a phone book, pull a London bus with my teeth, or in fact anything like that and that they simply handed over the award without asking for proof of my strength, but I assumed that I'd been selected for it on account of all the strenuous dancing I like to do at my concert performances.

It was not until much later that evening when I returned home and took a proper gander at the trophy, an ultra modern glass and steel affair, that I realised all was not well. The motto engraved upon the trophy 'America's Strongest Man' contained a small typographical error and actually read 'America's Strangest Man'!!

I contacted the organisers of the event first thing the following morning to alert them of their lexical unfortunacy and was horrified to be informed that there was in fact no mistake and that moreover the selection committee had in fact voted me 'America's Strangest Man' unanimously and that I had beaten all the other contenders hands down.

I was particularly annoyed by this because I'd had new sequins sewn onto my great big fluffy Gorilla costume specifically with the occasion in mind and had also, in the interests racial of harmony, decided to make my acceptance speech in a mixture of Urdu, Chinese and Walloon.

Anyway, hope you are well,
        Michael

A Word about Jesus

They have us stand in line here, in the cafeteria.

    The line snakes around the empty tables back out along the hall and into the street. We wait for them to roll up the shutters, we wait for someone to man the register, we wait for them to feed us and every day we wait for somethin to happen.

Church Bells in America

Last night I dreamt that Elvis dug up my front yard. Boy was I angry.

'Don't worry about it man,' he said. 'Tonite it's Free 'n' Easy. We'll all be dancin to Aubrey and the Beancurds then there's a film for us about fishing and free cigarettes. Then there's Snooker. That's a band by the way, Lamar, not a game.'

One day all the church bells in America will ring out for my Mary and me. They're only dreams now, only nightmares. Nothin ever happened.

I never saw anythin and there was nothin ever for me to stop. He shouldn't have done it. He's a just a child, a very talented kid. But he shouldn't have done it.

It ain't right and it never will be.

Mary

But I still miss Mary.

Just the other day she came into the cafeteria where I was eatin my lunch alone. She looked at me as she walked toward me, and I smiled at her.

'Hi,' she said and went on. It wasn't much, but somehow I know we'll be friends again before too long.

And when we are, I'm goin to tell her that she was right and I was wrong.

Mike's Roofing

More than anything I miss the animals.

We decided on Mike's Roofing for the side of the van. Not very imaginative I know, but simple and to the point. I wanted Mike's Roofing Services but it looked like MRS on the business card. Lisa suggested MJ's Roofing but I didn't want the J. I didn't want people to know or to guess at what I had been or have them making assumptions about me.

High up on a roof on a clear blue day is a good place to think, and sometimes when I'm three storeys up, re-laying a set of ridge tiles or re-pointing a chimney, I do think back and I do miss it all, but Doncaster, or at least the bit of town where me and Lisa live, is a nice place, and we have some good friends here.

I dress down these days; coveralls for work, shirt and slacks at the weekends. I keep my kneepads for roofing now, and sometimes when nobody's looking, I wear just the one glove.

Gold

Michael trudged along the path, crushed by the weight of his pack.

'Where is the gold?' he asked the pines, the thistles, the poison weed and the empty sunless sky.

'Where is the gold?' he cried in a quavering falsetto voice.

A group of Indians encountered him at Blackwater Lake, which lies between the Cariboo and the Skeena country.

'Where is the gold?' he asked and they could not tell him. He grew angry when they inquired, instead, if he wished for food.

'I'm not a bit worried,' he told them, ''coz when I open my mouth music comes out.' And on he trudged, still asking, 'Where is the gold?'

When he reached the Stikine River he asked again

and the Tlingit Indians told him that the goldfields were still another thousand miles away.

Michael pitched his tent on the riverbank and waited for a night to fall. It fell.

He hanged himself from the crosstree of his tent and left behind a hastily scribbled note.

Bury me here where I failed.

Acknowledgements

I am indebted to Pierre Berton's wonderful book *The Klondike Fever* for its descriptions and underlying narratives of the 1898 Gold Rush and also to J. Randy Taraborrelli's compellingly authoritative *Michael Jackson: The Magic and the Madness*, for other facts and details.

Versions of 'Gold' and 'Smart Dave Is Dead' were first published in *The Flash* and 'Goodbye' was included in *Vice* Magazine, The Fiction Issue 2008.

I would like to thank my wife Lorraine, Victoria Hobbs, Tina Jackson, Ben Yarde-Buller, Jack Slater, Mark Callaghan and Dan Rhodes, Esq. for their encouragement and support.